As Mattie lay in the dark, she found herself wondering if her intense feelings for Jake could pose a threat to the surrogacy. It was foolish to think this way when she knew they had no real future, but she couldn't help it. She'd never dreamed that she could meet someone like Jake before the baby was born.

And yet here she was, wishing at times that she could keep her body for him.

But in reality, if she was to have a man in her life at this point in time, she needed someone who would be there for her no matter what—not a gorgeous, dangerous playboy.

She needed a man who was prepared to share her with the baby she carried—someone prepared to wait. Unfortunately, Jake Devlin couldn't tick a single box in her list of vital requirements.

BABY STEPS TO MARRIAGE...

**A brand-new duet by RITA® Award-winning author
Barbara Hannay**

*Pregnancy is never predictable, and these two stories
explore the very different experiences of two friends,
Mattie and Lucy. Follow their steps to marriage
in these two very special deliveries...*

EXPECTING MIRACLE TWINS

Mattie Carey has put her dreams of finding Mr Right
aside to be her best friends' surrogate. Then Jake Devlin
steps into her life. He's cheeky, charming, intriguing
and gorgeous—but it's *so* not the right time
for her to fall in love...

THE BRIDESMAID'S BABY

Old friends Will Carruthers and Lucy McKenty are
thrown together again as best man and bridesmaid at
Mattie and Jake's wedding. Their biological clocks might
be ticking—but a baby is the last thing they expect!

EXPECTING MIRACLE TWINS

BY
BARBARA HANNAY

MILLS & BOON®
Pure reading pleasure™

First published in Great Britain 2009
Harlequin Mills & Boon Limited,
Eton House, 18-24 Paradise Road, Richmond, Surrey TW9 1SR

© Barbara Hannay 2009

ISBN: 978 0 263 20812 2

Set in Times Roman 10½ on 12¾ pt
07-0709-46888

Printed and bound in Great Britain
by CPI Antony Rowe, Chippenham, Wiltshire

Barbara Hannay was born in Sydney, educated in Brisbane, and has spent most of her adult life living in tropical North Queensland, where she and her husband have raised four children. While she has enjoyed many happy times camping and canoeing in the bush, she also delights in an urban lifestyle—chamber music, contemporary dance, movies and dining out. An English teacher, she has always loved writing, and now, by having her stories published, she is living her most cherished fantasy. Visit www.barbarahannay.com

CHAPTER ONE

MATTIE was grinning as she turned into the driveway at her new address. She couldn't believe her good luck. The block of flats was so much nicer than she'd expected, with charming whitewashed walls, Mediterranean-blue doors and sunny balconies that overlooked the bay.

Her flat—number three—was on the ground floor, which meant she wouldn't have to climb too many sets of stairs in the later months of her pregnancy, and Brutus would be able to run in and out to the garden to his heart's content.

As she parked on the driveway, she saw a welcoming pot of bright pink geraniums beside the doormat and the garden was filled with sunshine. Mattie could already picture her life here. In the mornings, she would bring her laptop outside and watch the sun sparkle on the water while she worked. She could put Brutus on his lead and take him for walks along the path beside the bay.

The flat was close to the hospital and it had all the right vibes. If she stood on tiptoe, she could even see the tip of Sydney Harbour Bridge. She was going to love living here for a whole year.

Everything about her new venture felt good. She'd talked to the doctors at length and she'd thought about the project from every angle, and she knew she was doing the right thing.

It was green lights all the way and, if all went well, by the end of the year she would deliver to her best friends the precious baby they both longed for. All she needed now was a successful implantation and the surrogacy would begin.

Humming happily, Mattie reached for the door key in her handbag, scooped up Brutus from his basket and opened the car door.

Wham!

A blast of strident music burst like a machine gun from number three and Mattie's happy smile disintegrated. Stunned, she checked her key tag, but there was no mistake—number three was definitely the right flat—*her* flat. Gina had assured her for the hundredth time when she'd handed over the keys this morning.

'It's yours for as long as you need it,' she'd said.

Everything was arranged. Gina's brother Will owned this flat, but he was working on a mine site in Mongolia and, as Mattie had refused any kind of monetary exchange for the surrogacy, Gina had settled on the use of the flat instead.

The last thing Mattie had expected was to find another tenant here, playing music—loud heavy metal music that set her teeth on edge. She clutched Brutus more tightly as she stared at the blue door.

Had squatters moved in? Were they throwing a party?

She almost returned to the safety of her car, but her sense of justice prevailed. She'd been assured many times that this was *her* flat. Gina and Tom were excessively grateful that she was willing to help them in their quest for a baby. Justice was on her side.

Mentally gathering her courage, she marched up the path, up the two stone steps and knocked.

And knocked.

And then thumped with her fist.

At last the volume of the music was lowered and the door opened, and Mattie took a hasty step backwards.

The man who suddenly filled the doorway did not look like a squatter. Far from it. But he did look like a pirate.

At least, that was Mattie's first thought, which was no doubt prompted by his rather wild dark hair and his scruffy jaw—and the fact that his shirt was unbuttoned to reveal rather a great deal of dazzling tanned chest. Mattie tried very hard not to look at his chest, but it was an incredibly eye-catching sample of male anatomy.

He propped a bulky shoulder against the door frame and studied her from beneath disconcerting half-lowered lids, and he managed to look both annoyed and bored by her intrusion. 'How can I help you?'

When he spoke, Mattie stopped thinking about pirates. For a moment she stopped thinking altogether. His voice was rich, dark and smooth, like an extremely sinful chocolate dessert. Combined with his gaping white shirt, it sent her mind completely blank.

She forced her gaze up and away from his chest and looked him bravely in the eye. 'I…um…think…there's been a mistake.'

A dark eyebrow lifted lazily. 'I beg your pardon?'

Mattie tried again. 'There seems to have been some kind of mix-up.' She waved her door key. 'This is my flat. Number three. I'm supposed to be moving in here today.'

He cast a quick, assessing glance that took in Brutus, curled in her arms, and her little car, crammed to the roof with her worldly possessions. Then he glanced back over his shoulder into the living room and, for the first time, Mattie saw his companion—a long-legged blonde, reclining on the sofa with a glass of wine in her hand.

'What's she want?' the woman called.

Ignoring her, the fellow narrowed his eyes at Mattie. 'Did the real estate office send you here?'

'No.' She straightened her shoulders. 'I have a…a private arrangement…with the owner. He knows all about it.'

'Does he now? And would you mind telling me the owner's name?'

'Excuse me?' Mattie was incensed. 'What right have you to ask that? I can assure you, my claim on this flat is legitimate. Is yours?'

To her annoyance, he chuckled. Mattie almost stamped her foot and Brutus, sensing her distress, licked her hand. And then the woman on the sofa uncurled her long legs, set down her wineglass and joined the fellow in the doorway. She draped an arm around the man's massive shoulders. 'What's going on, Jake?'

'Just a minor border incursion.' The man, whose name, apparently, was Jake, watched Mattie with a look of faint amusement.

'A what?'

'A territorial battle,' he told the blonde without taking his dark diamond-bright gaze from Mattie.

An unwelcome ripple of heat fluttered over Mattie's skin. She glared at Jake for causing it, and deliberately turned her attention to his sulky companion and rattled the keys again. 'There's been an unfortunate mistake about the flat. I'm supposed to be moving in here.'

'When?' asked the other woman in a tone as unhelpful as her boyfriend's.

'Today. Now. This afternoon.' Mattie pointed to the number three on the tag. 'I have a key.' Again, she glared at Jake. 'Do you have a key? Or did you break in?'

His response was to fold his arms and favour her with a withering look.

In desperation, Mattie said, 'Look, I told you I have an arrangement with Will Carruthers.'

'Will Carruthers sent you here?' Jake's eyes widened with surprise. 'Why didn't you tell me that in the first place?'

Mattie was surprised too. 'Do you know Will?'

'Of course I know him. I work with him in Mongolia. He's my best mate.'

'Oh.' She gulped unhappily. 'So I suppose he knows you're here?'

'Absolutely. I'm on leave. I had a week in Japan and now I'm in Sydney for a week and Will insisted I use his flat.'

Mattie clung to the faint hope that Jake's week was almost up. 'When did your week start?'

'Day before yesterday.'

Deflated, she dropped her gaze to Brutus, and he made sympathetic doggy noises and tried to lick her chin. 'There's obviously been a mix-up with the times.'

She tried not to sound too disappointed, but if she and this Jake fellow both had a claim on the flat, and if he was here first, she supposed she had no choice but to find somewhere else to stay for the rest of this week.

She wondered despondently where she should start her search for accommodation. It would have to be somewhere cheap and she didn't know Sydney very well.

'Rotten luck for you,' chirped the girlfriend and she

grinned smugly at Mattie as she rested her chin posses-
sively on Jake's shoulder.

'You haven't explained how you know Will,' Jake drawled.

'I've known him all my life,' Mattie told him and it was
perfectly true. Even though she hadn't seen much of Will
Carruthers in recent years, they belonged to a circle of
friends who'd grown up together in Willowbank in
Outback New South Wales.

'Will's sister, Gina, is my best friend,' she explained.
'And Gina and Will organised between them for me to live
here for twelve months.'

Jake frowned as he digested this and then he shrugged.
'In that case, I guess there's no reason why you can't move
in. After all, there are two bedrooms.'

His companion let out an annoyed huff.

Mattie's mouth opened and shut, then opened again.
She really didn't want to have to start searching for somewhere else, and this pair would only be here for a few
more days. 'Are you sure you don't mind? I don't want
to intrude.'

He uttered a gruff sound of impatience. 'I've offered,
haven't I? Anyway, I don't plan to be around much.' He
turned to the girl. 'We may as well hit the town now, Ange,
while—' He paused and gave Mattie the briefest flicker of
a smile. 'What's your name?'

'Matilda Carey.' She held out her hand rather primly.
'Mostly I'm called Mattie.'

'Jake Devlin,' he said, giving her hand a firm shake.

'Pleased to meet you, Jake.'

He indicated the small, silky terrier-cross in her arms.
'Who's this?'

'Brutus.'

Jake chuckled. 'Oh, yeah, he's a real brute, isn't he?' Then he remembered his companion. 'This is Ange.'

Mattie smiled at her. 'How do you do?'

'Oh, I'm fine,' Ange responded sulkily.

'Would you like a hand to bring your things inside?'

Jake's courtesy surprised Mattie, but its effect was offset by the predictably dark look on Ange's face. 'Oh, heavens, no,' she assured him. 'I can manage easily. I only have a canary cage and a few suitcases.'

'A canary?' Jake looked both amused and puzzled. He scratched his head and the gesture caused all sorts of muscles in his chest to ripple magnificently.

Mattie was about to explain that she'd inherited the canary from her grandmother but, once again, his chest distracted her.

'Jake.' A warning note had entered Ange's voice. 'We're heading off now, right? I'll get my things.'

'Sure,' he said and he began to close the buttons on his shirt.

Mattie watched as the two of them hurried away to find a taxi and then she went into the flat. It wasn't quite the exciting introduction to her new home that she'd pictured. The unpalatable music, although diminished, still throbbed from the stereo and she quickly switched it off.

She crossed the lounge room, skirting the coffee table with the abandoned wine bottle, bowl of nuts and glasses, and went through to the kitchen. The sink was littered with dirty dishes and the dishwasher door hung open, as if someone had intended to stack it but had been distracted by a better idea.

Down the hallway, she found the bathroom and she was not surprised to see wet towels dumped on the floor, as well as a pair of black lace knickers. Mattie had shared flats before and some of her flatmates had been untidy, so she was more or less used to this kind of scene. It was weird, then, that the sight of those knickers depressed her.

The next room was a bedroom, dominated by a king-size bed—unmade, of course. The bed's tangled sheets told their own story, as did the empty champagne bottle on the bedside table.

An inexplicable hollowness in Mattie's stomach sent her hurrying on till she came, at last, to a neat bedroom at the back of the flat.

It was much smaller than the main bedroom and there was no view of the bay, but it was perfectly clean and tidy.

And mine, Mattie thought. That was something. Actually, when she gave it further thought, she realised that she would probably have taken this room for herself anyway, and kept the front room with the view for visitors.

Then again, she mused, mulling over this as she headed back to unload the car, she probably wouldn't have too many visitors this year. Gina and Tom would want to visit from time to time and so would her parents, now that they'd recovered from the shock of hearing what she planned. But she'd agreed with Gina that they should keep their surrogacy arrangement very private, so she'd told her other friends very little about her move to Sydney.

Mattie's decision to move to the city had not been made lightly. She and Gina had talked it over at length. They both knew that if she'd stayed in Willowbank, they couldn't possibly keep the surrogacy under wraps. And Gina had been sensible enough to recognise that her constant vigilance of Mattie's pregnancy would be stifling, so they'd agreed it was better this way.

In some ways, however, it was going to be a lonely year. That was the one thing that had concerned the psychologist when she'd explored Mattie's motivations and commitment to the surrogacy process. Mattie had managed to convince her that she was perfectly happy with her own company. As a children's book author and illustrator, she was used to spending long hours lost in her work.

'Do you have a partner? A boyfriend?' the psychologist had asked.

Mattie had told her there was no special man in her life. She didn't add that there hadn't been a special man in her life for almost three years.

'What if you meet someone in the next few months?' the other woman had prompted. 'A pregnancy will restrict your social life.'

Mattie had thought it best not to mention that her social life had been on hold for quite some time. 'It's only one year out of my life,' she'd said with a shrug.

'But you're going to need support.'

'The baby's parents will come to Sydney for regular visits,' she'd responded with jaunty confidence. 'And my friends and family are only a phone call or an e-mail away.'

She'd wisely avoided announcing that she hadn't asked for support, but the truth was that Matilda Carey made a habit of giving support to others, rather than receiving it. Her impulse to help and rescue had begun so far back in her past it was as vital to her nature as her heartbeat—and that wasn't going to change in a year.

It was past midnight when Mattie heard the front door open and the sound of heavy footsteps on the terracotta tiles. She expected the murmur of voices or laughter, but all she heard was a thump and a muffled curse, as if someone had tripped, then more footsteps and, eventually, taps turning on in the bathroom.

The footsteps continued on to Jake's bedroom and Mattie pulled a pillow over her head. If those sheets were going to be tangled again tonight, she didn't want to listen to the sound effects.

She was washing up her breakfast things when Jake stumbled into the kitchen next morning, bleary-eyed and unshaven—like a bear with a sore head, her mother would have said.

'Morning,' Mattie said breezily, flashing a careful smile over her shoulder.

He replied with a grumpy monosyllable.

'There's tea in the pot and it's still hot, if you'd like some.'

Jake shook his head and scowled at the sparkling clean kitchen benches. 'What's happened to the coffee plunger?'

'Oh, it's up here.' Mattie reached into the overhead cupboard where she'd put the plunger pot after she'd washed it last night.

She handed it to him and he scowled at it as if he didn't recognise it. 'Did you wash this?'

'Well…yes.'

He scowled some more. 'And you've cleaned up the kitchen.'

'I didn't mind. It didn't take long.'

He shook his head and winced and she wondered if he had a headache. She thought about offering to cook bacon and eggs. Most guys seemed to find a big breakfast the best cure for a hangover.

But this morning she had the distinct impression that Jake Devlin would bite her head right off if she made such an offer. And, anyway, he had Ange to fuss over him, didn't he? She supposed his girlfriend was still in bed, sound asleep after her late night.

'I'll get out of your way,' she said. 'I'm going into town. I have an appointment this morning.'

Jake flashed a brief, keen glance in her direction. 'So have I.'

'Right.' Mattie inhaled sharply, surprised that he'd shared even this much about himself. 'I…um…hope it goes well, then.'

He looked faintly amused and, for a moment, she thought he was about to smile and say something friendly, but then he shrugged and turned his attention to the kettle.

Mattie hurried away and told herself that she didn't care if he was unsociable. He would be gone in less than a week and it didn't matter if he never smiled. His grumpiness was his problem, not hers.

But, as she went past the open bedroom door, she caught sight of those sheets again. She quickly averted her gaze— she didn't want to spy on Ange. Except…

She couldn't help taking another hasty glance and she realised then that she wasn't mistaken. The bed was empty. Clearly, Ange had not come home with Jake, which perhaps explained his bad mood.

CHAPTER TWO

THE woman at the nursing home smiled at Jake. 'Come this way, Mr Devlin. Roy's up and dressed, ready and waiting for you. He's very excited about your visit.'

'Glad to hear it,' Jake replied, but a small coil of dread tightened in his stomach as he followed her down a narrow hallway. This place was as bad as he remembered from his last visit. It smelled like a hospital and the walls were lined with pastel paintings of butterflies, flowers and fruit bowls. Roy wouldn't like them. Not a horse or a gum tree in sight.

As Jake passed doors, he caught glimpses of white-haired old folk in bed asleep, or nodding in their arm-chairs, and his feeling of dismay settled like cold stones in the pit of his stomach. He hated the fact that a great man like Roy Owens, who'd spent his entire life on vast Outback cattle stations, had to spend his twilight years shut away in a place like this.

His throat was already tight with emotion even before he entered Roy's room. But then he saw his old friend.

It had been six months since Jake's last visit and the changes in Roy were more devastating than ever. The tough and wiry hero Jake had idolised throughout his boyhood had all but vanished and had been replaced by a pale and fragile gnome. Jake tried to swallow the fish bone in his throat but it wouldn't budge.

Throughout Jake's childhood, Roy had been the head stockman on the Devlin family's isolated Outback cattle property in Far North Queensland. Until a few years ago, Roy had been a head taller than Jake's father and as strong as an ox. He'd taught Jake how to ride a horse and to fish for black bream, how to leg rope a calf, to fossick for gold, and to follow native bees back to their hives.

At night, around glowing campfires, Roy had held young Jake entranced as he spun never-ending stories beneath a canopy of stars. No one else knew as much about the night sky, or about bush lore, or the adventures of the early Outback pioneers. By the age of ten, Jake had been convinced that Roy Owens knew everything in this world that a man ever needed to know.

Roy could turn his hand to catching a wild scrub bull, or leading a search party for a lost tourist, or baking mouth-watering hot damper in the coals of a campfire. Most miraculous of all, Roy had endless patience. No matter how busy he'd been, or how hard he had to work, he'd always found time for a small lonely boy whose parents had been too occupied raising cattle, or training their racehorses, or pursuing their very active social lives.

When Jake had questioned his parents about Roy's transfer to a Sydney nursing home they'd claimed that they hated that he had to go away, but they had no choice. Roy needed constant care and regular medical checks.

'But have you visited him down there?' Jake demanded. 'Have you seen what it's like?'

'Darling, you know how terribly busy your father and I are. We will get down there, just as soon as we can spare the time.'

So far, his parents hadn't found time.

But Jake's affection for Roy had never wavered. It pained him that the old stockman, who'd been like a second father, was now a frail and lonely old bachelor with no family to support him. It tore at Jake's guts to see him waiting docilely in his postage-stamp-size room. He was fighting tears as Roy's face broke into an enormous smile.

'Jake, how are you, lad? It's so good to clap eyes on you.' With a frail hand Roy patted a chair. 'Take a seat, son. They'll bring us morning tea in a minute. Come and tell me all about Mongolia.'

Roy's body might have betrayed him, but his mind was still alert and, unlike most people who asked Jake about Mongolia, he was genuinely interested. He knew that horses were as important to the people there as they were in the Outback. And in the same way that many Outback kids learned to ride when they could barely walk, so did children on the steppe.

Roy was more than happy for Jake to retell the same stories he'd told last time. But, as Jake talked, he was painfully aware of the reversal of their roles. Now he was the one spinning stories and Roy was the grateful listener.

Two hours later, however, as Jake re-emerged into fresh air and sunshine, he knew that a few stories had not been enough. He was plagued by a gnawing certainty that he was letting the old guy down.

Mattie was in a very good mood when she came home from the doctor's. Everything for the surrogacy was set to go. Gina and Tom's frozen embryos had already arrived at the clinic and in two weeks' time, when Mattie's cycle was right, she would begin taking pre-transfer hormones. With luck on her side, she would be pregnant within a month.

She could hardly wait to get started.

Gina and Tom were an amazing couple and if anyone deserved to be parents they did. They'd been childhood sweethearts and their deep love for each other had remained unshakeable. These days they ran a farm on the banks of Willow Creek and Gina's house was always warm and welcoming, always filled with baking smells, a pot of tea at the ready. But there was a little yellow and white room at the end of the hallway, still waiting for the baby Gina longed for.

Mattie had seen Gina on the day she'd been told she needed a hysterectomy. She'd found her friend huddled in an unrecognisable ball in a corner of the lounge, red-eyed and shrunken—shut down—as if someone she loved with all her heart had died.

Of course, that was what had happened really, because now the baby Gina dreamed of would never have the chance to live.

For Gina, of all people, this was the cruellest blow. Mattie and Gina had been planning their families since they'd played with dolls in the tree house Gina's dad built.

Mattie was an only child and she'd thought two children would be nice, but Gina came from a big family and she had been adamant she wanted five. Her husband was *always* going to be Tom and they would have two sets of twins and then a single baby at the end, a baby girl for her to spoil and cuddle when all the twins had gone to school.

It was unthinkable now that Gina couldn't have at least one baby, and as Mattie had dumped any dreams of a family of her own after the truly toxic break-up with her fiancé, she hadn't taken long to come up with her surrogacy proposal.

For her it was a perfect solution. Gina and Tom could have their baby, and she had the chance to do something positive and life-affirming—the perfect antidote to heartbreak.

This way, Mattie figured, everyone was a winner and she'd wasted no time before putting the idea to Gina and Tom.

They'd invited her for Sunday lunch, a simple, relaxed, happy meal of roast chicken and winter vegetables, followed by berries and ice cream. After the other guests had gone, Mattie had stayed behind to help with the cleaning up. The three of them had been in the kitchen, Mattie washing wineglasses at the sink while Gina stacked the dishwasher. Tom had just brought in freshly chopped wood for the fire.

At first Gina hadn't understood.

'A surrogate pregnancy,' Mattie had clarified.

There'd been a momentary flash of shock in Gina's face, but it was quickly outshone by hope and excitement. Then Gina had seen her husband's grim frown and doubt had crept into her eyes.

'That's a huge ask, Mattie,' Tom had said. 'Have you thought this through? You'd be carrying another woman's baby, fathered by another man.'

'I know, I know. But you're both my best friends.'

Tom had tried to smile and failed, and he ran a distracted hand through his spiky red hair. 'I can't get my mind around the fact that a woman other than Gina could give birth to my child. That's off the wall. Even when it's a wonderful friend like you.'

That discussion had taken place six months ago.

Mattie had thought the subject was dropped and she'd been disappointed. The idea of carrying her friends' baby had filled her with a sense of purpose, which she badly needed. After the break-up with Pete she'd cared for her grandmother but, since Gran had passed away, her life had felt…blank and not very meaningful.

She'd kept busy, of course, had created another book and that had been fun and worthwhile, but she'd still felt vaguely restless and empty. And then Gina and Tom had called.

Could they come around for a chat? Tom had changed his mind. They'd considered adoption, but it wasn't their first choice and if Mattie really was still willing to carry their baby they'd be deeply and eternally grateful.

Now, in Sydney, after receiving the doctor's reassuring news, Mattie was in the mood for a minor celebration, and she stopped on the way home and bought a bottle of wine. After all, she wouldn't be able to drink any alcohol once she was pregnant. She also bought the ingredients for one of her favourite meals, a scrumptious potato and mushroom pizza.

If Jake Devlin was still in an irritable mood, or if Ange was hanging about the flat, giving out sour looks, she would ask them to share the pizza. It was amazing how often a nice meal cheered people up.

Back at the flat, she sent a quick, excited e-mail to Gina and Tom and then she took Brutus for a nice long walk. She was extra-patient when he wanted to sniff at interesting smells every few metres or so and when she got back, happily windblown and refreshed, she put one of her own CDs in the player—a very popular movie soundtrack.

She opened the wine and poured a glass, which she sipped while she sifted flour and kneaded dough and chopped vegetables for the topping.

The pizza was almost ready for the oven when she heard the sound of a key in the front door. Her skin flashed hot and cold.

For heaven's sake, it was such a silly reaction. What was the matter with her? As Jake Devlin's footsteps sounded in the hallway she concentrated on adjusting the oven's temperature setting, but she knew it wasn't the stove's heat that made her face bright and hot when he came into the kitchen.

'How's it going?' he asked casually.

Mattie flashed a nervous smile in his direction. He looked as devastatingly sexy as ever.

'Fine,' she said.

'You've been busy.'

'Not really.' She tried to sound offhand. 'I've made plenty of mess, but it's just a pizza.'

He came close—*too* close—and stood looking down at the pizza, with his hands resting lightly on his lean hips. Today his shirt was respectably buttoned and there was absolutely no reason for Mattie to feel weak at the knees.

While Jake studied her pizza with surprising interest, she drew a calming breath. At least, her deep breath was supposed to be calming but it didn't seem to help her. She was still distinctly fluttery.

'That looks really good.' He spoke with every appearance of sincerity. 'I've never seen potato used on a pizza.'

'Oh, you should try it. It's delicious.'

Great. Now she sounded breathless.

'I'll bet it's terrific.' He smiled at her and his smile was more dangerous than his bare chest had been.

Mattie's movements became jerky and nervous as she began to tidy the cooking mess. Without looking at Jake, she said, 'It'll be ready in twenty minutes.'

'I'm afraid I can't hang around that long. I've already made plans.' He slipped his sleeve cuff back and glanced at his wristwatch. 'I have to leave again almost straight away, and I need to shower first.'

Mattie smothered her ridiculous disappointment with an extra-bright smile. She supposed Jake was going off to meet Ange.

'Enjoy your dinner,' he called over his shoulder as he left the room.

'I will.'

It was a warm evening so Mattie ate her pizza slices and drank another glass of wine out on the balcony with Brutus at her feet. The balcony faced the east, but the sky reflected the pinks of the sunset from the western sky and the light turned the water a pretty pearlescent grey. She enjoyed the meal immensely—despite the dull cloud of tension and disappointment that had settled over her.

She was very annoyed with herself for feeling low. Yesterday morning she'd been over the moon with excitement about living in Sydney alone. This evening she longed for company.

It didn't make sense. When she'd started preparing this meal, she hadn't really expected to share it with anyone and the sudden slump in her spirits was irrational. How would she cope with nine months of pregnancy and the ups and downs of her hormones if one unpleasant man she hardly knew could send her moods swinging like a seesaw?

She didn't even like Jake Devlin!

Her low spirits lingered as she went back inside, cleaned up the kitchen and covered the canary's cage. She asked herself disconsolately, *What now?*

Of course, there was one thing that she could always

rely on to lift her mood. She fetched her art block, pens and paints and set them on the coffee table.

Humming to herself, she found a flat cushion, then sat cross-legged on the floor, ready to sketch an opening scene for her new book.

The idea for this story had been bubbling inside her for the past few weeks, but she'd been too busy planning her move to get started. This evening was the perfect time to let her ideas for the artwork come to the surface and spill onto the page. At last.

As always, her children's story would start in her young heroine's ordinary world—an old-fashioned house in an inner-city suburb, where the little girl lived with her mother and father, her cat and a canary.

In this new book, Mattie would begin with a bathroom scene.

She selected a pencil and sharpened it carefully, took a deep, happy breath and made the first mark on the fresh white page. Within moments, she was completely absorbed, lost in the enchanting world of her imagination. Thank heavens it never let her down.

The flat was in darkness when Jake arrived home some time after midnight. Last night he'd tripped over something in the dark, so he turned on a light this time and he blinked as the living room came to life, blinked again when he saw the clutter on the coffee table.

Surely Mattie, the neat freak, hadn't left this mess?

Curiosity got the better of·him and he moseyed over to take a closer look.

Blow me down.

The table was covered by a painting, which Mattie had

obviously left to dry. It was a pen and ink sketch, coloured with pretty watercolours in a soft wash, and it showed the corner of a bathroom.

A little girl peeped out of a sea of bubbles in an elegantly curved, claw-footed bathtub. Bright rainbow-tinted bubbles drifted over the edge of the bath and onto a white fluffy mat on the floor, where a pair of pink-and-white-striped socks with lacy frills lay abandoned.

The long sleeve of a blue jersey hung over the edge of a wicker laundry basket and the cheeky face of a black cat peeked out from behind the basket.

It was such a simple little scene, drawn with an economy of lines and coloured delicately, but there was something utterly fascinating about the picture. Jake looked again at the little girl's mousy-brown curls and beady blue eyes and he chuckled softly. She looked incredibly ordinary and yet unexpectedly appealing. Not unlike her creator.

Mattie woke next morning to the unexpected sound of pots and pans being rattled in the kitchen, and when she opened her bedroom door she caught the distinctive aroma of mushrooms frying.

She'd slept in, after staying up much longer than she'd intended last night. When she'd finally finished work on her painting she'd lain awake for ages, thinking about the rest of her book, but she hadn't heard Jake come in, so he must have been very late. How extraordinary that he was up already.

She dressed quickly, pulling on a T-shirt and jeans, and she made a hasty stop in the bathroom to wash her face and tidy her hair, then she entered the kitchen cautiously.

Jake was whisking eggs and he turned and grinned at her. 'Morning.'

'Good morning,' she returned carefully.

'I let Brutus out into the garden,' he said.

'Thanks.' She blinked with surprise when she saw that he'd also filled Brutus's bowl.

'How did such a tiny mutt end up with a name like Brutus?' Jake asked as he watched the little dog crunch miniature biscuits.

'I've no idea,' Mattie admitted. 'I guess his former owners had a sense of humour, even if they were careless.'

'Former owners?'

'I have a good friend, Lucy, who's a vet. Someone dumped Brutus on her doorstep and she needed to find a new owner.'

Jake stopped whisking eggs. 'And you offered.'

'Yes.'

For a long moment, Jake watched her with the slightest hint of a smile lurking in his eyes, then he pointed to the frying pan. 'I found some leftover mushrooms in the fridge so I'm making an omelette.'

He looked rather pleased with himself, but Mattie refused to be amused or impressed. Last night she'd been shocked by her reaction to this man and she'd vowed to remain un-impressed by anything about Jake Devlin. With a little will-power, she could rise above the attraction of his broad manly chest, his sexy smile and his flashing dark eyes.

There was simply no point in getting hot and bothered about him. Apart from the fact that he already had a girl-friend, or possibly several girlfriends, he brought back memories of the one time she'd fallen disastrously in love and she'd vowed never to put herself through that kind of agonising heartache again.

Besides, no matter how attractive Jake was, he would

be gone in under a week. And, very soon after that, she would be pregnant with someone else's baby.

No man on earth would be interested in her then.

Not that she minded. This was her year for living chastely. She was dedicated to a higher cause, to Gina and Tom's baby. When she was old and she looked back on her life, she would see this gift to her friends as one of her greatest triumphs.

With a breezy wave of her hand, she smiled at Jake. 'You're welcome to the mushrooms.'

'Would you like to share this omelette?'

'No, thanks. I'm allergic to eggs.'

He shot her a sharp, disbelieving glance and Mattie shrugged. 'I usually have oatmeal.'

He looked momentarily disappointed, and she couldn't suppress a spurt of triumph. *Touché, Mr Devlin.*

But then he gave an offhand shrug. 'Bad luck for you. My omelettes are legend.'

As Mattie spooned boring oatmeal and water into a bowl and stuck it in the microwave, she asked, over her shoulder, 'So where did you learn to cook?'

'In Mongolia, on the mine site.'

She turned to him. 'Really?' In spite of her vow of indifference, she was intrigued.

'We have this fabulous cook—a French Canadian called Pierre—and, whenever I'm at a loose end, I pop into the kitchen to lend him a hand.'

'I don't suppose there are too many ways to spend your free time on a mine site in Mongolia.'

'Not unless you can get a lift into the capital, Ulaanbaatar.' Using a spatula, Jake skilfully folded the omelette in two.

'Are you a geologist like Will?'

He shook his head. 'I'm an enviro.'

'What's that?'

'An environmental scientist.'

'So it's your job to make sure the mining companies don't wreck Mongolia?'

He grinned. 'More or less.'

'I guess that must be rather satisfying.'

'It's not a bad job.' Jake lowered the heat beneath his frying pan.

The microwave pinged and Mattie gave her oatmeal a stir.

'What about you?' he asked casually. 'What do you do?'

'Oh, I haven't been to university, and I don't have what you could call a career. I tend to drift from one situation to another.'

'But you paint.'

'Well…yes. I suppose you saw the mess I left last night. Sorry.'

'Don't apologise. I was actually glad to see stuff lying about. Now I know you're normal.'

His sudden smile was so charming that Mattie felt a dangerous flutter inside and she was grateful when a burst of song from the cage by the window distracted them both.

She darted across the room and removed the cover from the cage. 'Morning, Pavarotti.'

Jake snorted. 'Pavarotti?'

'That's his name. Like the opera singer.'

He shook his head as he skilfully tilted the pan so that the omelette slid smoothly onto a plate.

At the cutlery drawer, Mattie fetched him a knife and fork and got a spoon for herself, and then they sat opposite each other at the small kitchen table—and Mattie knew she was in trouble.

Her insides were twittering in time with the canary's warbling.

Jake nodded towards the bird cage as he cut into his light and fluffy omelette. 'So you're a fan of opera?'

Remembering the heavy metal music he'd played, she almost said yes, just to provoke him, but her habitual honesty prevailed.

'My gran was the opera fan,' she explained. 'She named the canary. I wanted her to call him Elvis, but he was her bird so of course she had the last say.' Mattie realised that further explanation was necessary. 'My grandmother died last year and I inherited Pavarotti.'

Jake nodded slowly. 'You were close to your grand-mother?'

'Oh, yes. I lived with her and looked after her for the last two years of her life.'

Across the table, his dark eyes registered surprise and then, eventually, an unexpected sadness. He scowled and looked more like the gruff man Mattie was used to and the flutters inside her settled. She was much more comfortable soothing other people's worries than dealing with her own fluttery insides.

They ate in silence for several minutes. Eventually, Mattie said, 'Do you have something interesting planned for today?'

'I was thinking of taking in a movie.'

'On a lovely day like this?'

His jaw stuck out as if he didn't appreciate her implied criticism. 'I've missed six months' worth of movies. I've a lot of catching up to do.'

'Of course.'

'Do you want to come?'

The question was so unexpected that Mattie's mouth gaped unbecomingly. Her mind whirled. She wanted to ask Jake if Ange was his girlfriend. Or was he a free agent who hooked up with the nearest available woman whenever he was on leave?

She didn't have anything planned for the day, but if there was even a slim chance that Jake was actually asking her on a date, she should say no.

'I'm afraid I can't come today,' she said quickly and decisively, before she could be tempted to change her mind. 'I have another appointment.'

If Jake was disappointed he didn't show it, but after he'd gone Mattie sunk to a new low. She couldn't believe how restless and just plain miserable she felt. The flat felt hollow and empty and she seemed to rattle around inside it—like a pebble in a tin can.

In a bid to think about something else—*anything* else besides Jake Devlin—she rang around the local hairdressers until she found one who had a cancellation.

Two and a half hours later, she grinned with delight at her reflection in the salon's mirror. Chestnut and copper streaks had transformed her mousy hair, and an elegant bob flattered her jawline and gave a nice emphasis to her cheekbones.

She told herself she was doing this as a pre-pregnancy ego boost. The new image had nothing to do with Jake. But when she got back to the flat, she took a long bath and she changed into her best dark grey trousers and cream silk blouse and she put garnet studs in her ears.

She looked fabulous, but she felt foolish. Wouldn't Jake wonder why she'd dressed up?

She was still trying to decide if she should change again when she heard the front door open, so she dived into the kitchen and pretended to be busy in the pots and pans cupboard.

Jake came down the hall, then paused in the doorway. 'Excuse me,' he said, a small smile playing at the corners of his mouth. 'I think I'm in the wrong flat.'

To Mattie's eternal embarrassment, she blushed.

'I guess you're going out?' he said. 'You're all dressed up.'

'Yes,' she lied. As she closed the cupboard door, she hoped he couldn't see through her fat white fib. 'I'm meeting a friend for dinner.'

Jake nodded slowly, then said quietly, 'Have a good evening.'

'I will. Thanks.'

He was about to head down the hall when he turned back. 'By the way, Mattie.'

'Yes?'

'The new hair looks fabulous.'

She was really mad with herself as she set off on foot down the street. Ever since she'd met Jake she'd lost her grip on her common sense. Now, she'd lied about her plans for this evening and here she was, wandering the streets of Sydney like a lost waif, looking for somewhere to eat. The really silly thing was she'd stocked the refrigerator with the ingredients for a perfectly good supper.

She decided to eat at the first place she found—a café a block away. It was a simple place with bare concrete floors, metal tables and chairs and selections of Asian-style noodles and stir-fries scrawled in chalk on blackboards.

Most of the customers were wearing jeans and T-shirts

and Mattie felt distinctly overdressed, but she took a seat and was determined to enjoy herself.

She placed her order and asked for a glass of white wine and all went well for about ten minutes. Then Jake strode in.

CHAPTER THREE

MATTIE'S heart began a ridiculous thumping. Jake was dressed in black and his unruly hair was tousled by the wind as he stood at the café's front counter. Framed by the doorway, shoulders back and feet planted wide apart, he looked unbelievably gorgeous.

She wasn't sure if he'd seen her, but it could only be a matter of moments before he did, and even if she could come up with a plausible explanation, he'd probably realise that she'd lied about meeting a friend. Talk about embarrassing!

His dark eyes scanned the café and she quickly dropped her gaze, letting her smooth new hairstyle swing forward, hoping that it would hide her face. Perhaps she could pretend she hadn't seen him.

Within a heartbeat, however, strong, confident footsteps rang out on the concrete floor, and they stopped at Mattie's table. Holding her breath, she lifted her head and there he was, standing before her.

He looked directly into her eyes and he smiled.

Mattie swallowed. What could she say? It would be pathetic to trot out a feeble excuse about her friend being delayed. Somehow, she just knew that Jake would expose her as a fraud.

While she sat there, feeling silly, Jake held out his hand. 'How do you do?' He smiled with effortless charm. 'I'm Jake Devlin. Do you mind if I join you?'

She expected to see a teasing glint in his eyes but, to her surprise, she could only find genuine warmth. Nevertheless, she hesitated.

'Come on, say yes,' Jake urged. 'Otherwise you'll force me to try my pick-up lines.'

'Are they corny?'

'So bad you could feed them to chickens.'

His confession was accompanied by a lopsided self-deprecating grin that melted Mattie on the spot. She suspected that Jake had seen right through her, but it somehow no longer mattered. He was wiping their slate clean. Starting again. And she was enchanted. Caught. Hook, line and sinker.

'You're welcome to sit here, Mr Devlin.'

'Thank you.' He pulled out a chair and sat opposite her and happiness fizzed inside Mattie like soda pop.

Following his lead, she held out her hand. 'How do you do? I'm Matilda Carey.'

'Pleased to meet you.' Jake's expression was deadpan. 'Do your friends call you Mattie?'

'Quite often.' She gave a little shrug and added rather recklessly, 'At times they've been known to call me Florence Nightingale.' She didn't mention the other tag that she hated—Saint Matilda.

'Is that accurate? Are you a caring type?'

''Fraid so.'

The skin around his eyes crinkled and he cocked his head on one side. 'Let me guess. You're probably the kind of girl who cares for sick grannies.'

Mattie's sense of fun faltered. Was he teasing her? Uncertain, she quickly changed the subject. 'I've already ordered. I'm having the chicken noodle soup.'

'I think I'll try the beef stir-fry.' Jake waved to a waitress and, when she came over, he gave his order. 'And I'll have a beer.' Turning to Mattie again, he asked, 'Would you like another glass of wine?'

She tapped the side of her glass. 'This is fine.'

When the waitress left, Jake leaned towards Mattie, hands linked on the table top. His smile faded and, with it, all pretence dropped away. 'Seriously, Mattie, I've been thinking about what you did for your grandmother. That was a huge gesture, to spend two years looking after her.'

She took a quick sip of her wine to cover her surprise, then set the glass down.

'Did it feel like a big sacrifice?' he asked urgently.

'Not at all. Those two years were rather lovely. Gran was always so sweet. So grateful for my company. She never complained about her health.'

'Was she very ill?'

'She had a weak heart, so she tired easily and she couldn't take proper care of her house, but I was happy to help.'

'What do you reckon would have happened if you hadn't looked after her?'

'She'd probably have gone into a nursing home. My parents run a hardware store in a little country town and they were too busy to give her the care she needed.'

'They were lucky you stepped up to the plate.'

'I was happy to help,' she said again. 'Anyway, it was tit for tat. When I was little, my gran nursed me through the chickenpox and the measles and umpteen bouts of tonsillitis. Mum was always too busy helping Dad in the store.'

Unexpectedly, Jake frowned and he looked deeply pained as he rearranged the salt and pepper shakers in the middle of the table.

'What's the matter, Jake? Have I said something wrong?'

He let out a heavy sigh. 'No. You're just confirming my worst fears.'

'Really? How?'

Exhaling another deep sigh, he rested his chin on his hand, and suddenly he was telling her about an old stockman he knew, someone from his childhood called Roy, who was now in a nursing home here in Sydney. As Jake talked about how strong and tough this stockman used to be and how shockingly weak and shut-in he was now, Mattie could see how deeply he cared for the old man.

'My parents and I have let him down,' he said quietly. 'We should be doing more for him.'

On impulse, Mattie reached out and touched the back of Jake's hand. He stiffened as if she'd burned him.

'It sounds as if you've visited Roy whenever you can,' she said softly. 'There's not much else you can do if you're working in Mongolia, but I'm sure your visits mean a lot.'

His gaze met hers and his dark eyes were shimmering and vulnerable and something shifted inside her, almost as if a key had been turned in a lock. *Oh, help.* She'd been trying not to like Jake Devlin, but now she feared she was beginning to like him very much.

Too much. Was she falling in love?

Surely not. She mustn't fall in love. Not again. Not ever. Certainly not now.

Gently, she removed her hand from his. 'Did you take Roy with you to the movies today?'

'No.' Jake looked angry as he shook his head. 'I didn't

even think of it. How selfish am I? Roy would have loved a movie. It was an action-adventure flick and they're his favourite.'

'There's always tomorrow,' Mattie suggested gently.

His brow cleared. 'Yes, of course. It's my last day, but that's a good idea.'

'Actually,' Mattie said, warming to this subject, 'if Roy's an outdoor type, he might prefer to be out in the fresh air. You could take him on a ferry ride on the harbour. Do you think he'd be well enough for that?'

'I reckon he might be. That's a *really* good idea.'

The waitress brought Jake's beer and Mattie couldn't help watching the movements of his throat as he took a deep draught. Every inch of him seemed breathtakingly male and dark and sexy. She was beginning to think she'd never met such an attractive man.

Apart from her fiancé, the guys she'd dated had all lived in her home town and she'd known them since they'd first grown baby teeth. She'd gone to kindergarten and school with them. They'd belonged to the same pony club and Sunday school. There were no mysteries there.

Jake, on the other hand, was a man surrounded by mystery.

Pink rose in Mattie's cheeks and Jake watched the telltale colour with mounting dismay.

His reasons for following her to this café weren't crystal clear to him, but he supposed he'd been hoping for useful tips on how to help old Roy. One thing was certain—he wasn't here because she looked cute in those sleek grey trousers, or because her new hairstyle looked terrific and brought out the blue in her eyes.

Hell, no. He wasn't interested in Mattie as a *woman*.

She wasn't even close to his type. She was small and

serious and mousy. Well, maybe she wasn't mousy exactly, certainly not now, but she was most definitely small. And *earnest*.

The heat that had scorched him when she'd touched his hand a few minutes earlier was *not* what he'd first feared. He couldn't possibly have experienced hot, pulsing *lust* for her.

On the other hand, Jake didn't want to think too hard about why he'd ended it with his latest female companion, Ange, or why he'd started hanging about the kitchen in the flat in the mornings, or why he'd casually asked Mattie to the movies today.

None of his recent behaviour made sense, and Mattie was giving out confusing signals too. It was as if she was trying to impress him and avoid him at the same time and, like a fool, he'd followed her here. He wasn't in the habit of following women, but he'd convinced himself that she would be able to give him good advice about Roy. That was the only reason he'd come here, wasn't it?

He wished he felt surer. It was a relief when their meals arrived and he could concentrate on eating.

Mattie declared that her soup was delicious—so full of noodles and vegetables that she ate most of it with chopsticks.

Which caused a tiny problem. Jake found himself watching the way she deftly used the chopsticks. Her hands were pale and delicate and graceful, possibly the prettiest hands he'd ever seen. He pictured her holding a pen or a paintbrush as she created her whimsical works of art.

He thought about the way she'd touched him a few minutes ago. Imagined—

'What's the food like in Mongolia?' she asked.

Jake blinked, dragged his mind into gear. 'Er…do you

mean the traditional food of the locals, or what we eat on the mine site?'

'Both, I guess.'

'Our cook serves mainly western food, but the Mongolians eat mutton. Loads of mutton. They even drink the mutton fat. It's no place for vegetarians.'

Mattie wrinkled her nose. 'I rather like Mongolian lamb.'

'The meals in Asian restaurants here in Sydney are nothing like the mutton eaten out on the steppe.'

Mattie accepted this with a shrug. 'Do you live in barracks, or one of those little round tents?'

'I have a tent. They call it a *ger*.'

'It sounds rather primitive.'

'Actually, *gers* aren't too bad. The walls are made out of layers of felt and they're quite snug. In winter we have a stove for heating and in summer we can roll up the sides for ventilation.'

'It's a very different world, isn't it?' she said, glancing out through a window to the city lights.

'That's part of the attraction for me. Then again, I grew up in a remote part of the Outback, so I suppose that made it easier for me to fit in.'

Her blue eyes challenged him. 'Why do you work there?'

Jake had been asked this question before, but suddenly, when Mattie asked him, he wished he had higher motives. There was no point, however, in trying to pretend he was a paragon of virtue.

'I'm footloose and fancy free,' he said, aware that his jaw was jutting at a defensive angle. 'And the job offered a chance to see a really different part of the world. But the big drawcard is that it pays very well.'

He expected to read disapproval in her eyes. To his

surprise, she smiled. 'And when you're on leave you can party hard.'

'Mostly.'

The obvious fact that he'd been partying when Mattie had arrived on his doorstep and the equally obvious fact that he was nowhere near a party right now was not something Jake wanted to analyse too closely.

'Tell me more about your paintings,' he said quickly to change the subject.

Mattie dismissed this with a graceful wave of her hand. 'They're just illustrations for a children's book.'

'Do you plan to write the story as well?'

She nodded.

'Have you been published?'

'Uh-huh. I've had three books published so far.'

'No kidding?' He knew his eyes were wide with surprise. 'That's terrific. I've never met an author.'

'Most people don't think of me as a *real* author. They assume that children's stories are incredibly easy to write.'

'How could they be easy, when they're created entirely out of your imagination? And you don't just write the stories, you do the illustrations as well. Aren't children supposed to be the harshest critics of all?'

She nodded and smiled, clearly pleased by his enthusiasm.

'What are your stories about?'

Now Mattie looked embarrassed. 'Nothing you'd be interested in.' She poked her chopsticks into the noodles at the bottom of her bowl.

'Try me.'

'Don't laugh,' she ordered.

'Wouldn't dream of it.'

'They're about a little girl called Molly.' Carefully, she

laid the chopsticks across her bowl and sat back, arms folded.

'And…' Jake prompted.

'Molly's actually a white witch and, when her parents aren't looking, she has all sorts of adventures. She goes around doing secret good deeds and terrific acts of heroism.'

Just like her creator, Jake thought, and suddenly he was struggling to hide his amusement.

Mattie's eyes blazed. 'I knew you'd laugh.'

'I'm not laughing.' Why couldn't he stop smiling? 'Honestly. I'm seriously impressed. I'm sure Molly's stories are very popular.'

'They seem to be.' Mattie sniffed, then rolled her eyes, as if she hoped he would drop the subject.

To make amends, Jake said quickly, 'Would you like to go somewhere for coffee?'

She almost glared at him. 'Don't you have other plans?'

Across the table their gazes met, and held. Mattie's eyes were very blue and steady and Jake had the distinct impression she was about to decline his invitation. Which was wise, wasn't it? After all, they weren't planning to hook up. To go on somewhere else for coffee implied taking another step—in completely the wrong direction.

Before he could think of a way to extricate himself from this trap of his own making, Mattie smiled slowly.

'Coffee sounds good,' she said and her smile deepened, revealing an enchanting dimple. 'Your place or mine?'

He couldn't help returning her smile. She was cleverly letting him off the hook, placing them back on their correct footing. As flatmates. For one more day.

'Try my place,' he said smoothly. 'It's very handy—just around the corner.'

A breeze was blowing in from the harbour and it buffeted them as they walked home, making it hard to talk. When they reached the flat, Brutus was as eager to see Jake as he was to see Mattie. Jake laughed as he gave the little dog a scratch behind his silky ears.

Mattie offered to get the coffee started, but she wasn't at all surprised when Jake announced that perhaps he would go into the city for a bit, after all. She wasn't surprised, but she was disappointed, which was utterly silly. She knew she didn't want to get involved with him. But she also knew she was the kind of girl men left behind when something better came along.

She waved him off with a bright smile. 'Have a good evening.'

'You too.'

'And if you take Roy out tomorrow, I hope you have a good time.'

'Thanks.'

Jake paused on the front step and looked back at her as she lifted a hand to hold back her windblown hair. She twisted a strand lightly around one finger and tucked it behind her ear. There was nothing flirtatious about the gesture, but Jake seemed to be transfixed. His gaze scalded her as he stared at her hand, and then at her hair, at her ear.

His interest was so intense that Mattie couldn't breathe. She swayed against the door frame and her legs threatened to give way. She'd never really understood what swooning involved, but she was certain that if Jake had touched her at that moment she would most definitely have swooned.

But Jake gave a slight shake of his head and the possibility vanished. 'Would you come?' he asked.

'Pardon?' Mattie felt dizzy and confused. What was he

asking? Surely he wasn't inviting her to go out with him for a fun-filled night on the town?

'Tomorrow,' he said with a smile. 'When I take Roy out, will you come too?'

Whoosh! It was like having a bucket of cold water dumped on her head. A chilling dash of reality. Now Mattie knew without a shadow of a doubt that Jake hadn't followed her to the café tonight because he liked her new hairdo, or the way she looked in her best silk blouse. He hadn't shared a table with her because he fancied her.

And he wasn't interested in taking her out now. The unflattering truth was—Jake was the same as everyone else in Mattie's life—he needed her help.

Sooner or later, everyone turned to Mattie Carey for help, but this time, for her emotional health, she knew she must say no. She shook her head. 'Sorry.'

He frowned at her. 'Don't tell me you have another appointment. What is it this time? A manicure?'

She looked down at her hands. 'I…I need to get on with my book.'

'Couldn't you spare just one day, Mattie?'

His dark eyes were shining with sincerity, but she refused to be taken in. After one meal with him, she was already a mess. If she spent a whole day in his company, she would fall completely under his spell, and that was unwise. It was worse than that. It was ridiculous. Perilous.

She'd tried one long-distance relationship and she was still flinching at the memory almost three years later. She never wanted to embark on another, especially not now when she was on the verge of becoming pregnant with someone else's baby.

'It would be a pity if you couldn't make it,' Jake said,

watching her closely. 'I know Roy would really enjoy your company.'

At the mention of Roy she started to weaken. Poor old fellow. Was she making a mountain out of a molehill? Jake was simply asking for help to entertain an old man. How could she try to read romance into that?

And, after all, helping people was what she did best.

Behind her back, she crossed her fingers and hoped she wasn't making a really bad mistake. 'All right,' she said. 'I'll come for Roy's sake.'

As soon as Jake left, Mattie spread out her art things and started on another illustration for her book. This was to be a double-page spread and she wanted to create a scene with Molly at her bedroom window, looking out at the city at night.

She would show Molly and her cat silhouetted against the yellow light of the bedroom window. There would be houses dotted through the night, all with brightly lit windows. Through the windows, she would show glimpses of people who needed Molly's help. A sick child, a lonely old woman, a lost kitten.

In her head, Mattie knew exactly how this illustration should look, but tonight something wasn't gelling. She couldn't slip into the 'zone'—into the happy, creative space that usually cocooned her from the rest of the world while she lost herself in her work.

Tonight Jake Devlin-size thoughts kept intruding. She couldn't stop thinking about him, kept seeing the way he'd looked at her when she'd innocently fiddled with her hair. She was sure she'd never forget the heart-in-mouth connection she'd felt, as if they were suddenly, perfectly in tune.

She was sure that if she'd been any other girl Jake would

have kissed her then, but of course he hadn't. Instead, the astonishing vibe that passed between them had remained unacknowledged. And there wasn't much point in trying to read anything into it. Even if there had been a momentary spark with Jake, Mattie had learned not to trust such feelings.

For years she'd wondered if she would ever fall in love. There'd been a high school crush, but that had only lasted one term before she'd been unceremoniously 'dropped'. She'd taken a long time to get over that blow to her self-esteem and, in the years that followed, she'd dated the occasional local boy but there'd been no one special.

Then, three and a half years ago, a hot-looking stranger had arrived in Willowbank.

Pete from Perth had a cute smile and he'd ambled into her parents' hardware store and set his cap at Mattie and swept her completely off her feet. She'd been crazy about him and when he'd returned to Western Australia she'd taken the long flight over there to stay with him. She had done this every month for seven months and Pete had helped to pay for her fare. She'd felt very worldly and sophisticated. And needed.

Pete had promised her the world...well, a diamond ring and a white wedding, a house in the suburbs plus two children...which was everything that Mattie had wanted. But then the day had come when Pete had rung from Perth and Mattie had heard the difference in his voice.

Something had happened.

When he'd suggested that the air fares to Perth were too expensive for her to keep flying over, it had been dead easy to start putting two and two together. But she'd been too scared to ask the crucial questions. She hadn't wanted to hear the answers.

Finally, however, Pete had sent her a text message:

Sorry, I need to check out of this wedding. It's not you, baby, it's me.

She'd rung back in a blind panic and heard the truth she'd desperately feared. Yes, he'd found someone else and could she return the engagement ring by registered mail?

That had been nearly three years ago.

Mattie's heart hadn't just broken, it had shattered and bled. And she'd felt such a loser. So ashamed. Ashamed that she'd fallen for a guy so cowardly he'd called off his wedding via a text message.

And she was ashamed that everyone—yes, literally *everyone* in Willowbank—had known about her wedding plans. From the mayor down to the butcher's apprentice, the whole town knew she'd been dumped. Not only had her pride been hurt, however. She'd lost faith—in men, in herself, in the romantic twaddle everyone called love.

Her friends had tried to tell her that she shouldn't see this as a failure. Easy for them to say. They hadn't been a hair's breadth from happily-ever-after and then discarded by remote control.

Mattie thought it was perfectly reasonable that she'd given up on her foolish dream of a husband and family. Utterly logical that she'd retreated from the dating circus and hadn't had a boyfriend since. It was far safer to care for people and find countless ways to be helpful than to risk another train wreck for her heart.

Next morning, however, Mattie was pleased she'd agreed to visit Roy. She took one look at his twinkling blue eyes and she liked him instantly. He had thinning hair, carefully combed over his sun-spotted scalp, a wiry body and thin legs, bandy from a lifetime spent astride a horse, but there was something lived-in about him that made her feel very comfortable as they shook hands.

Impulsively, she gave him a hug. Then she saw the shining joy in Roy's eyes when he greeted Jake, and a fresh coil of happiness warmed her heart.

'You must be keen to get out of here, mate,' Jake told Roy lightly. 'You came bolting out of that door like a race-horse out of the starting gate.'

'I didn't want to waste a minute.' Roy's pale blue eyes were shining with the wicked glee of a schoolboy planning to skip school. 'The nursing mafia ganged up on me,' he told them. 'They reckon I can only stay out for two hours.'

'What happens if you're not back in time?' Jake asked. 'Do you turn into a pumpkin?'

'More likely Prince Charming.' Roy laughed and gave Mattie a wink.

He wasn't walking too steadily, and she quickly offered her arm for support as he made his way to the car.

'Thank you, sweetheart,' he said, but then he shot a gimlet glance Jake's way. 'How did a black-hearted rascal like you find this lovely lass?'

Mattie held her breath and watched Jake's face. She wondered how he would answer this. He would be as keen as she was to make sure that Roy didn't jump to the wrong conclusion about them. He was unlikely to say, Oh, Mattie turned up on my doorstep. Or, We're sharing a flat. But how else could he explain?

She needn't have worried. Clearly, Jake was more prac-tised at coming up with smooth answers to awkward ques-tions than she was. 'Mattie and I met through a mutual friend,' he said with a slow smile that did not include her.

'One of my mates from Mongolia comes from the same country town as Mattie.'

'Where's that?' Roy asked and Mattie silently congratulated Jake for managing to steer the conversation in a safe direction.

'A little town called Willowbank,' she told him. 'West of the Blue Mountains.'

Roy was delighted. 'So you're a country girl.'

'Born and bred.'

'I knew it.'

Roy might have waxed lyrical about the superior charms of country girls, but they'd reached the car. Mattie suggested that Jake should drive and that Roy should have the front passenger seat because it was easier for him to get in and out, and she insisted that she was perfectly happy in the back.

As Jake drove out of the nursing home's carefully manicured grounds he said, 'Mattie and I planned a ferry trip on the harbour, but I don't think we'll have time for that if you only have a couple of hours. Is there somewhere else you'd like to go?'

They'd emerged onto the busy main road and Roy peered through the windscreen at the expanse of red-roofed houses with television aerials and powerlines. He squinted at the busy lanes of traffic zooming up and down. 'I don't s'pose there's a park nearby? Somewhere with a little patch of bushland?'

'Sure to be,' Jake asserted confidently. 'We'll keep our eyes peeled.'

'If all else fails, we could go to the Botanical Gardens,' Mattie suggested. 'But, I must admit, I don't know much about the parks here. I'm not very familiar with Sydney.'

'Now, if you were looking for pubs,' said Jake, 'I'd be your man.'

But they were in luck and they found a leafy park quite quickly.

Pleased with themselves, they helped Roy out of the car, and the old man stood with his hands on his hips and looked about him at the smooth sweep of lawns dotted with picnic tables and chairs, at the gas-fired barbecues and big shade trees, carefully pruned to give a clear view beneath them. He looked at the ornamental lake, where young mothers and toddlers were feeding ducks. Then he tipped his head back and stared up at the clear blue sky and drew in a deep breath.

'What do you reckon?' Jake asked with a hopeful smile.

Roy looked about him again and he nodded slowly. 'It's nice.'

Mattie could see the wistful sadness in his face.

'But it's not what you hoped,' Jake suggested carefully.

Roy's face pulled into a worried grimace. 'It's…it's all very tidy, isn't it?'

Mattie laughed to ease the tension. 'You want proper bush—straggly gum trees with fallen branches and knee-high dry grass, don't you, Roy?'

He smiled sheepishly. 'S'pose I do.'

'And you want to be able to smell eucalyptus leaves.'

Roy nodded.

'And to boil a billy over a campfire.'

'Don't get carried away, Mattie,' Jake warned, signalling frowning looks over Roy's head. 'There's no way we can do all that here.'

But Mattie was already thinking ahead. This was her very favourite situation. She was never happier than when she detected a need in someone—an almost impossible need—and then figured out a way to meet it. The impulse had begun as a game when she was very young—anticipating a simple need her mother might have, like knowing, without being asked, whether to pick beans or peas from the garden.

It had been easy for Mattie because she knew her mother's habits—beans with beef and peas with lamb—but her mother would exclaim with delight when she discovered the peas in the colander, already shelled, or the beans topped and tailed.

'My amazing little mind-reader,' she would say and sometimes she would hug Mattie, making her feel loved and secure and needed.

'I'm going to scout around for gum trees,' she told Roy and Jake. 'You guys sit over at that picnic table and I'll be back in two ticks.'

Halfway along the path that circled the ornamental lake, she found a clump of gum trees and she knew the familiar skinny white trunks and dull khaki-coloured tapering leaves would gladden Roy's heart. Soon she was back with an armful of fallen twigs and gum leaves.

Jake was smiling and shaking his head at her. He looked puzzled. Roy looked delighted.

'They've dried out but they still smell good,' she told Roy as she dumped them on the slatted timber table top.

With a shaking hand, Roy reached out and picked up a twiggy branch. He crushed the brittle gum leaves between his fingers and leaned in to smell the distinct aroma of eucalyptus. 'Perfect,' he whispered with a blissful sigh.

'It's only a little way around the lake to see them,' Mattie said. 'And I think we can organise billy tea too.'

'No way,' Jake protested. 'We can't have an open fire in a public park.'

Mattie laid a placating hand on Jake's arm. Big mistake. High-voltage tension zapped through her. She retracted her hand, took a shaky breath.

'I...I know we can't have a fire here.' Her voice was thready and soft. She took another breath and told herself that this morning was all about Roy. Her focus was Roy. Jake was a minor distraction she must ignore. 'But we could boil a billy over a camping stove at our place,' she said. 'And we can even stir the tea with a gum tree twig. That would be authentic enough, wouldn't it, Roy?'

Roy was looking a tad dazed, trying to keep up with Mattie and with the undercurrent humming between her and Jake, but he nodded happily.

Jake, however, was still protesting. 'But we don't have the gear.'

'We can stop off at a camping store on the way home. It'll only take a minute to buy a little stove and a billy and they're dirt cheap.'

Jake shook his head but his eyes were warm as he smiled at her, and she could feel that warmth all the way to her toes.

CHAPTER FOUR

JAKE had to hand it to Mattie.

Single-handedly, she had given Roy a perfect two hours. The old guy had been deliriously happy, ensconced in an easy chair in their front garden with Brutus snuggled in his lap, while Jake boiled a billy on a small gas ring.

The morning had been filled with laughter and a huge sense of fun, part of which involved making the billy tea with as much formal ritual as a Japanese tea ceremony.

Summoning immense dignity, Roy threw a handful of loose tea leaves into the pot. Mattie gave the brew a flourishing stir with the mandatory gum tree twig and Jake swung the billy in a wide arc to mix the brew, pleased that he hadn't lost the knack.

They drank their tea out of tin mugs, which Mattie had found in the camping store, and they ate scones, which she'd bought from a bakery and warmed in the microwave, serving them liberally smothered with butter and golden syrup.

'Next time I'll make you proper damper,' she assured Roy.

Jake wanted to tell her that she needn't worry about next time, that Roy wasn't her responsibility. But he sensed the advice would be water off a duck's back for Mattie Carey. She'd taken Roy under her wing in the same way she'd saved Brutus from the animal refuge, and she'd cared for her grandmother and, no doubt, countless other people.

It was clearly the way Mattie was wired. She bent over backwards to please people, to find ways to make them happy. Jake wondered how many people went out of their way to make her happy. Who went to great lengths to make her face light up with the same happiness and amazement he'd seen in Roy this morning?

By the time Roy returned to the nursing home, he was a very different old man. He was walking more confidently and grinning from ear to ear, and Jake could have sworn he saw more colour in his face.

But it came as a shock to realise that Roy wasn't the only guy who'd changed in Mattie's company. Jake felt different too. This morning, buzzing about Sydney in her little car, hunting down camping stores and mucking about with that tiny gas ring, he'd felt more relaxed than he had in years. He'd been more optimistic too, less cynical and not nearly as self-absorbed.

He really liked the person he became when he was around Mattie. He was beginning to think that if he'd had more time, he would like to get to know her better, to let their acquaintance deepen into friendship. Not that he was in the habit of developing friendships with women.

His time in Mongolia was so unbearably long and his leave so annoyingly short that he usually spent most of his leave trying to meet as many different women as possible. A deep and meaningful friendship with one woman was not and never had been on his agenda.

Meeting Mattie, however, had thrown him off balance. He was sure he should do something about that, but he had no idea where to start.

'That was fun, wasn't it?' Mattie punctuated her comment with a happy sigh as they headed back into the city, with Jake still behind the driving wheel. 'Roy's a darling.'

Jake chuckled. 'He'd be red as a tomato if he heard you calling him a "darling". As far as I can remember, he's always been shy around women.'

'A lot of those Outback guys are.' Mattie shot him a cheeky sideways glance. 'Present company excluded.'

Jake shrugged this aside. 'Roy certainly took a shine to you.'

'Maybe…but he's *very* fond of you, Jake.'

'Yeah…well…I guess he looks on me as the son he never had.'

'That's nice.'

The tone of Mattie's voice made Jake glance at her. Her smile had turned inward, as if she was thinking about something personal, something that made her pensive and slightly wistful.

When the silence lingered, he wondered if he'd said something to upset her. He'd merely mentioned that Roy looked on him as the son he'd never had… How had that plunged Mattie into such deep contemplation? Clearly, whatever absorbed her did not involve him.

To Jake's dismay, he realised he wanted her attention. Wanted her animated company. Wanted *her*.

There it was—the crazy truth.

Without making a single overt advance, Mattie had crept under his defences. She was so not his type and yet he was attracted. Madly.

He wanted to know more about her. Wanted to know everything, while there was time.

'Have you always gone out of your way to help people?' he asked.

She smiled. ''Fraid so.'

'I should have said people and animals,' he amended.

'Well, yes, it probably started with kittens.'

'Really? When was that?'

A reminiscent gleam crept into her eyes. 'Oh, I was about ten. There was a group of us who always used to hang out together. We'd play cricket, go swimming or riding and have picnics down by the river.'

'Sounds like fun.' Jake was thinking of his lonely child-hood on an Outback cattle station, with no brothers or sisters, only his busy parents and a string of indifferent governesses.

'One time, we went swimming in the local creek,' Mattie continued. 'And I found a bag of half-drowned kittens that someone must have dumped just before we arrived. I was devastated.'

A warm ache flowered deep inside Jake as he pictured ten-year-old Mattie, her blue eyes stricken by the pitiful plight of a bunch of kittens.

'I raced back to my place,' she went on. 'My parents weren't home—they were busy at their shop. So I quickly organised my friends, drying the kittens off with bath towels and feeding them bits of sardines soaked in milk. Then I hid them in the bottom of my wardrobe.'

'I hope you didn't try to keep them there.'

She made a scoffing sound. 'I was too smart for that. The next day I piled them into the basket on the front of my bike and pedalled them all over the district. I reckon I must have visited just about every family from Willowbank to Nardoo.'

'And you found safe homes for all those cats?'

'Every one,' she said with a grin.

Jake smiled too. 'So…what do you have planned for the rest of today?' he asked her.

Mattie blinked and bright colour rushed into her cheeks. 'Oh…um…I should be getting on with my book.'

'But you'd rather not,' he suggested, sending her his most charming smile. 'You'd rather come to the movies with me, wouldn't you?'

She didn't answer and Jake's spirits took a downward dive. She was sitting very still, staring directly ahead.

'I could throw in lunch as well,' he said.

'But we're very casually dressed.' She frowned down at her T-shirt and faded jeans.

'No worries. There's a terrific fish and chip joint just around the corner from the cinema.'

A corner of her mouth twitched, then her lips curved upwards into a fully fledged grin. She turned to him, offering a full-frontal view of her beautiful smile. Her blue eyes danced. 'How did you know I can't resist fish and chips?'

'I'm a deeply intuitive guy.'

'Sure.'

He pretended to be hurt. 'Haven't you noticed my sensitive side?'

Still smiling, she shook her head, but then, with the speed of a light switch, her smile vanished. 'This wouldn't be a date, would it?'

Jake felt the fun go out of his day. He stopped at a red light and turned to her. 'I simply want to thank you for helping out with Roy.' To his surprise, he found himself adding, 'But would it be so terrible if we went on a date?'

'Ange might think so. Won't she mind?'

At first, Jake thought Mattie was joking. What had Ange

to do with this? She was already a fading memory, joining the long list of other women he'd dated.

Mattie, however, was looking distinctly concerned.

'Don't worry about Ange,' he said.

'Have you broken up with her?'

'She wasn't really a girlfriend.'

Her mouth opened as if she was planning to say something, but then apparently changed her mind. As the lights changed and they took off again, she said, 'So…what movie are you planning to see?'

Grinning with relief, Jake bravely named a romantic chick flick that he knew was showing that week. He usually avoided them like the plague, but he was pretty damn sure it was the sort of film Mattie would love. Most girls did. And it was the least he owed her after this morning.

To his surprise, she screwed up her nose. 'I can't believe you want to see a soppy film like that,' she scoffed. 'I prefer crime thrillers. Any chance of catching a good one?'

He was sure she was just being Mattie, trying to do and say the right thing, but this time he wasn't going to argue.

Mattie sat in the popcorn-scented darkness, super-aware of Jake's presence beside her. She tried to concentrate on the screen—it was one of those complicated spy films where you needed to stay focused at the beginning or you'd be hopelessly lost—but Jake's proximity and the darkness were conspiring against her.

She was almost bursting out of her skin with lust.

Good grief. She felt as if she'd overdosed on hormones. How on earth was she supposed to sit still for almost two hours when Jake Devlin was so close?

She was terrified of making a fool of herself, of bursting

the bubble of happiness that had seemed to enclose them today. She'd had such a wonderful time this morning with Jake and Roy. And lunch had been perfect, eating crunchy fish and chips, sprinkled with salt and lemon juice, straight from the paper it was wrapped in.

Now, however, her lusty thoughts were making it impossible for her to relax and enjoy the movie. She kept stealing glimpses of Jake's hunky profile, lit up by the glow of the screen. He was gorgeous. She was deeply, helplessly attracted to him.

There, she'd admitted it. Whether it was sensible or not, it had happened, and her desire felt like a bushfire rapidly burning out of control.

She allowed herself to wonder how it would feel to trace the line of Jake's profile with her lips, to kiss his forehead and his dark brows, then his slightly beaky nose, his rough jaw and, finally, his yummy, sensuous mouth.

Crikey, she was really getting carried away. She tried again to concentrate on the movie. Jake might expect her to talk about it later. He might be the kind of movie-goer who liked to analyse and dissect the plot.

She'd told him that she hadn't wanted to see a romance movie, which was totally untrue. She loved them, but she knew guys would rather have their teeth drilled than watch soppy movies. Now, however, an unexpected romance was unfolding on the screen and Mattie found herself drawn in.

The spy had met a mysterious beauty, a brunette with a waiflike, vulnerable quality. Mattie decided she was almost certainly a double agent. It was obvious, wasn't it? Why couldn't the hero see that the woman wasn't telling him the whole truth? He was obviously smitten. Fool.

Half an hour later, Mattie had changed her mind about

the double agent. She was deeply absorbed in the film, desperate for the good guy to win and for the lovers to get
together, when out of the blue the lovely heroine started
her car and it exploded in a burst of garish flames and
flying metal.

Mattie screamed.

Jake reached for her hand and gave it a reassuring
squeeze. 'It's only a movie,' he whispered, nuzzling her ear
as he did so.

'A-a-ah…' It was the most articulate response she could
manage. The on-screen heroine might have gone up in
flames, but Mattie was on fire too. Her earlobe and the side
of her neck were burning from the gentle brush of Jake's
lips. Their arms were linked now and she was ablaze from
her elbow to the tips of her fingers.

Hot desire pooled in the pit of her stomach. Man! She'd
never felt so turned on.

A desperate sigh escaped her, but it sounded like a moan
and she blushed with embarrassment.

Thank heavens for the darkness.

Jake was still holding Mattie's hand when they came out of
the cinema. They both blinked at the bright daylight outside
and Mattie hoped Jake didn't expect her to recall every twist
and turn in the movie. For the entire second half she had been
unable to concentrate on anything except the mesmerising
pressure of his thumb gently stroking the back of her hand.

'So what did you think of that?'

'It was pretty good.' She held her breath, expecting
more questions.

He smiled at her and his dark eyes smouldered. 'Would
you like to go home now?'

Was this code for something else? Jake was still holding her hand and she felt as if so much had changed since they'd left the flat this morning. This was their last night together. Tomorrow, he was flying back to Mongolia.

'Home sounds good,' she said and she knew there was every chance she would have agreed if he'd asked her to swim across Sydney Harbour.

The short journey to the flat seemed to take forever and the whole way Mattie worried. Did Jake feel the same as she did? She was astonished by the force of her attraction for him. She thought she might expire if he didn't want to make love to her the minute they were inside the front door.

She thought briefly—very briefly—about her surrogacy plans. But that was in the future—almost a fortnight away—and Jake was only here for this one last night. Right now, at this moment, she only wanted to think about him. She wanted to stop being careful and to simply let go.

They parked the car and tension hovered above them like a private thunder cloud as they walked together to the front steps. Even before Jake put the key in the door, they could hear Brutus barking a greeting. The little dog jumped around their ankles and then darted outside to explore the garden.

Mattie dropped her shoulder bag onto a lounge chair. Jake set the keys on the coffee table. They looked at each other. His eyes were intense and yet warm. The muscles in his throat rippled.

'Mattie,' he said softly.

'Yes.'

He looked at her with a slightly puzzled smile. 'That sounded like an answer.'

'I think it is, Jake.'

He drew a sharp breath, but he didn't speak.

Mattie knew he was waiting. This was it—an all or nothing moment. Bravely, she said, 'I thought you might be asking if…if I'd like you to kiss me.'

Before she could say anything else, he closed the gap between them. With a soft sound that might have been a groan, he drew her in and kissed her.

Oh, *how* he kissed her.

His lips were as eager and scorching and greedy as Mattie needed them to be. In a matter of moments, she and Jake were stumbling down the hallway together, laughing a little with surprise that this was really happening, stopping to lean against the wall while they exchanged feverish kisses, stopping again while Jake's hands stole under her T-shirt, sending a rush of sweet anticipation over her already sensitised skin.

In the doorway to Jake's bedroom, however, Mattie froze.

'No, not in here,' she whispered. Not on those same sheets he'd tangled with Ange. 'Come to my room.'

With a soft wordless cry, he scooped her up and carried her down to the little back bedroom and together they tumbled onto the bed, hungry, urgent, eager.

Lips, hands, bodies sought each other—kissing, touching, nibbling, caressing.

Jake lifted Mattie's T-shirt over her head. She heard his swift gasp of surprise and she felt obliged to confess her secret weakness for low-cut sassy lingerie. But she didn't mention that she'd kept up the tradition even though there'd been no one to admire the effects.

He chuckled softly. 'I'm so glad you have a vice.' With reverent fingers, he touched the lacy trim on her bra. 'This is a weakness you should never, ever try to give up.'

Mattie was amazed by how uninhibited she felt with

Jake, as if being with him took her straight into her natural element.

She loved everything about making love with Jake. Loved the way he tasted and the way he smelled. She adored the daring ways that he kissed her and touched her, sometimes gentle, sometimes fiery.

Always, always he knew exactly what she needed and before she even knew that she needed it.

When they neared the point of no return, only one thing worried her. If Jake wasn't prepared, she would have to raise the touchy subject of protection. With the surrogacy about to begin, she couldn't afford to take any risks.

But she needn't have worried. Jake was well and truly prepared and he was as keen to avoid any risks as she was.

Later, as afternoon sun streamed through the window, Jake reached for Mattie's hands. He lifted them to his lips and kissed each of her knuckles. 'Has anyone told you that you have beautiful hands?'

She laughed with surprise and held out her hands so she could study them in the deepening sunlight.

'See how white and dainty they are.'

But Mattie was looking at Jake's big, wide hands and the darkness of his skin. She trembled deliciously as she remembered the incredibly intimate way his big hands had touched her.

'Compared with yours, my hands are tiny.' She giggled softly. 'To be honest, I prefer yours.'

'No, no,' Jake protested, his voice turning playful. 'Your hands are gorgeous.'

'Yours are gorgeous-er.'

'I could eat your hands.'

He began to nibble her fingertips and Mattie gasped as the warm intimacy of his teeth and tongue sent ripples of heat straight to the pit of her stomach.

'I...I suppose I should take more care of my hands,' she murmured. 'When my friend Gina was single, she used to slather cream on her hands every night and wear gloves to bed.'

Jake laughed. 'No gloves in this bed, please.'

'You won't know. You won't be here. You'll be in Mongolia for the next six months.'

'I'm here now.' Jake took her hands again and held them above her head. With a soft chuckle he lowered his mouth to hers. 'Make the most of me.'

'Oh, don't worry. I plan to.'

The magic afternoon rolled into an equally magic evening. Dusk fell, filling their room with purple shadows, and Mattie and Jake realised they were ravenously hungry. They went through to the kitchen to make pasta, deciding they would concoct a brilliant sauce from whatever ingredients they could find in the fridge and the pantry.

Together they investigated Will's collection of CDs and agreed on a middle-of-the-road rock 'n' roll number and, while the flat throbbed with its beat, they cheerfully chopped bacon and vegetables and supervised the pasta boiling on the stove. The whole time, their newfound happiness bubbled through them, erupting into sudden bursts of unexplained laughter or melting into blissful lingering kisses.

The meal turned out surprisingly well, and they found half a bottle of wine to wash it down. Then, knowing they had the luxury of one last long night ahead of them, they took Brutus for a walk.

Salty wind plucked at their clothes and at their hair as they walked hand in hand, stealing kisses and sharing jokes, grinning madly at the moon and feeling very much at one with the entire magnificent, beautiful universe.

It wasn't until Jake looked back on their behaviour the next morning that he realised they'd carried on very much like lovers. Like idyllic fairy-tale lovers who could look forward to a happy and long-lasting future. Not at all like a couple on a one-night stand.

It was a worrying discovery.

As dawn broke, he lay awake beside Mattie, fighting to resist the temptations of her delectable body and to hold at bay the tantalising memories of last night—the heady scent of her skin, the sweetness of her lips, the seductive sounds of her laughter and her soft whisperings.

Last night, every inch of his body had been on fire. He'd never spent a night like it, but now he needed to clear his thoughts, to sort out exactly what had happened to him and to Mattie and what it meant now. Had he made a terrible mistake?

His normal reaction to having bedded a new woman was a sweet feeling of conquest, a subtle boost to his ego that left him tingling with anticipation for repeat performances. But, last night, he'd experienced something more. So much more. And it left him this morning feeling quite shaken.

Making love with Mattie had been beyond beautiful, beyond amazing—but what had caught Jake completely by surprise was the deep sense of inner contentment he'd felt afterwards. He'd lain here, with this heavenly woman in his arms, and he'd been filled with an astonishing sense of well-being, a nudging awareness that Mattie Carey was completely and absolutely right for him.

The experience was totally new, and he found it more than a little frightening. He'd never felt this close to anyone since...

For a devastating moment he was a small boy again, locked on the outside of his mother's bedroom, afraid and lonely and lost. Understanding nothing...

No, he couldn't think about that or the following years when his mother had shut him out. He never allowed himself to think about it.

His priority now was to work out what to do about his worrying desire to stay with Mattie, to protect her.

To protect her from what, exactly?

It seemed he wanted to protect her from everything— falling buildings, colds and chills, other men...

Get real, Jake...

It was his usual style to put distance between himself and the latest girl, to keep her guessing. Normally, he would go surfing, or ring up a mate and down a couple of beers at the pub, anything to avoid getting too involved with any one woman.

Today he would be leaving Sydney and he knew he had to shake off this sense of deeper connection to Mattie Carey. He hadn't planned on starting a relationship. There was no point. He could never promise anything long term and it was only fair that Mattie understood that.

But it was too hard to think about this while lying beside her. Carefully, Jake eased out of bed without disturbing her. He padded down the hall to the kitchen, where Brutus was waiting to be let out. He opened the door and watched the little dog dash off into the garden.

He put water on to boil, removed the cloth covering Pavarotti's cage, topped up the bird's seed and gave him fresh water. While his coffee was brewing, he went to the bathroom to shower.

Naked, beneath the hot water, he thought about the tedious journey back to Mongolia—the long flight to Beijing, followed by another flight to Ulaanbaatar and then a journey by truck out to the mine site.

If he was honest, he had to admit that he'd never really minded his current lifestyle. Even though he'd complained at times about being stuck in Mongolia for long stretches, he quite liked the isolated blokeish world of the mine. It was almost an extension of his boarding school days.

He got on well with his workmates. They filled the long evenings with chess or poker, backgammon or Scrabble, and he'd also made friends with a few of the locals and managed to go horse-riding at least once a week.

He certainly liked the money he earned. Given the current mining boom and the constant need for environmental monitoring, anyone with his qualifications could make a small fortune if they were willing to work on the remote mines scattered around the world. Jake was prepared to do just that.

His ambitions were important to him, mainly because he had something to prove to his parents. OK—it was a clichéd young bull/old bull struggle, but he'd grown up determined to make his way in the world by rejecting the life his parents had planned for him.

His father had never had much time for him. Admittedly, Jake and his mother had been close before her breakdown, but from the age of nine, he'd been left in the care of a succession of governesses, or to be entertained by Roy. Then there'd been boarding school.

His parents had focused on raising their cattle and training their racehorses, or throwing lavish parties after race meetings. Jake had spent a solitary childhood, never feeling that his parents needed him, and in response he'd chosen to make his own way.

It was vitally important to prove to his parents that he could become successful in his own right, so he had no plans to change his job in the near future. But, this morning, the thought of going back to Mongolia for six long months left a chasm in his gut so big a truck could pass through it.

He was going to miss Mattie.

But he wasn't right for her.

He couldn't give her the steady commitment she needed and deserved. If he was halfway decent, he should tell her that. Now, this morning, before he left, before it was too late.

He was leaning against a kitchen bench, coffee mug in hand, when Mattie came in, wearing a white towelling bathrobe tied at the waist. Her feet were bare and she hadn't bothered to brush her hair. Jake wondered if she'd deliberately left her hair in that just-out-of-bed disarray because she knew it looked so damn sexy.

Her soft skin had a peachy sleep-warmed glow and he had to fight a fierce urge to pull her in for a deep and meaningful good morning kiss.

Hell. Hadn't he decided it was time to back off?

'Morning.' Mattie sent him a shy smile, then looked around the kitchen. 'Oh, I see you've taken care of Brutus and Pavarotti. Thanks.'

'No problem.'

Jake watched the upward tilt of her soft, full lips as she smiled again. He watched the way she tucked a wayward curl behind her ear and he forgot every one of his good intentions in his need to taste her, to let his hands slip inside her towelling robe to explore once more the exquisite softness of her slender waist, the silken roundness of her breasts.

Right at this moment, there was only one thing he wanted and that was to take Mattie straight back to bed.

His lips dipped to meet hers. Ah, yes…he could spend the whole morning just kissing her…

'Um.' Gently Mattie broke the kiss and she pushed her hands against his chest, easing out of his embrace. Her eyes were serious as she dropped a light kiss on his chin. 'I think I'll take a shower.'

'Sure,' he said, disappointed. 'Will I…er…start breakfast?'

She paused in the kitchen doorway. 'Don't you have to pack this morning?'

'I'll take two seconds to throw my few things in a bag.'

Mattie gave a shrug. 'Cook whatever you like, but don't worry about me. I'll fix tea and toast when I've showered.'

'Let me know if you'd like a hand in there.'

She smiled, but there was no coy come-hither message in her eyes and she left without replying.

Jake took a moment to collect his thoughts. He'd almost made a serious mistake, carrying on with Mattie like a lover, instead of a guy who was about to walk out of her life.

He'd never enjoyed the morning after, letting women know that they couldn't hope for a long term future. He'd had some bad experiences with women who were clinging and possessive and he supposed he should be pleased that Mattie was letting him off the hook so easily.

He should be very grateful. And he was. Of course he was.

CHAPTER FIVE

MATTIE was towelling her hair dry when she heard the phone. She'd been trying to decide if she should use the blow-dryer to try to turn her hair into the sleek bob the hairdresser had achieved, but she abandoned the challenge and hurried into the kitchen, damp hair in a tangle.

Jake had already answered the phone and, when he turned and grinned at her, her tummy flipped.

He was so beautiful. She longed to hurl herself into his arms, but he was leaving today and she had to be brave. The last thing he would want was a clinging vine.

'It's for you,' he said.

'Who is it?'

He handed her the phone. 'Your friend Gina.'

'Oh.' Mattie's stomach stopped flipping and tied itself in knots instead. If Gina had spoken to Jake, her friend would be agog with surprise and brimming with questions. Mattie took deep breath. 'Hi, Gina.'

'Mattie, how's life in stunning Sydney?'

'Stunning.'

'I'll bet it is.' Gina's voice was rippling with undertone. 'If the man answering your phone's deep, sexy "hello" is anything to go by, you've been having a *ball*! Crikey, Mattie, it didn't take you long to find Jake.'

'I didn't *find* him. He's a friend of Will's from Mongolia and he's been staying here this week.'

'Oh, I remember now. Will mentioned a friend called Jake. Bit of a ladies' man, I take it. Gosh, Mattie, has he been staying there in the flat with you?'

Mattie glanced over her shoulder to check if Jake was listening. He'd made scrambled eggs and now he was piling fluffy spoonfuls onto a piece of toast.

'It seems Will mixed up the dates, but it's worked out OK,' she said.

'So you've been sharing Will's flat with this Jake guy?'

Gina's own voice had risen by several decibels. By contrast, Mattie kept her tone deliberately calm.

'I just told you, Gina. It's worked out fine.'

From the other side of the kitchen, Jake winked at Mattie, then he pointed with his thumb to indicate that he was taking his breakfast out onto the balcony.

She waved to him and smiled her gratitude.

'Is he hot?' Gina asked.

'Yes, actually.'

'From what I've heard, he's dangerous.'

'Not really.'

'Oh, my God. You've fallen for him, haven't you?'

'Not fallen…exactly.'

'Oh, Mattie, you have. I can hear it in your voice. Oh, no! I know what this means. You're madly in love with this Jake guy and you want to marry him and have his babies and you don't want to do the surrogacy any more.'

'Gina, for heaven's sake, calm down. Of course I'm still going ahead with it.'

'Really? You're sure?'

'I'm absolutely sure. I couldn't be surer. Do you really think I could let my best friend down?'

'But will Jake mind when you're pregnant?'

'He's not going to know.' Mattie's hand tightened around the receiver. She lowered her voice to just above a whisper and prayed that Jake couldn't hear. 'He's going back to Mongolia today.'

'So you haven't told him about the surrogacy?'

'Of course I haven't. I promised you and Tom that I'd keep this completely private. Why would I discuss it with one of Will's friends?'

Right from the start, Mattie had planned to keep this project under wraps, but Tom had been particularly anxious that their plan must remain strictly secret. He'd been terrified they'd end up as a double-page feature spread in some women's magazine.

'But it must be hard to keep a secret from a boyfriend,' Gina said.

Mattie answered quite firmly. 'He's not exactly my boyfriend. I only met him a few days ago.'

'But you're involved with him, aren't you?'

Mattie gulped. She couldn't possibly answer that question. Gina knew her history with Pete and she would probably get defensive. Besides, it sounded so brazen to admit that she'd slept with a guy she'd only met a few days ago.

But it hadn't felt brazen. It had felt totally right and perfectly lovely.

She drew a quick breath. 'Everything's very…up in the air.' To her horror, her eyes filled with tears. 'Gina, I'll ring you tomorrow. OK?'

'I'm so sorry, Mattie. I just get so intense about this baby. Now I've got you crying.'

'I'm not. Honestly. But I've got to go now. I'll ring you soon. Or I'll e-mail. I promise.'

The tears began to stream down Mattie's cheeks as she replaced the receiver. She couldn't believe she'd dissolved so quickly. What if Jake saw her like this?

She hurried to the sink and splashed her face with cold water, snatched up a hand towel and mopped at her eyes. That was better.

She found a dollop of scrambled eggs in the pot on the stove and a piece of toast sitting in the toaster. She collected a plate, a knife and fork, helped herself to the food and took it outside to the balcony. For a couple more hours, until Jake was on the plane, she had to behave as normally as possible.

Jake had almost finished his breakfast when she arrived on the balcony. He was watching her closely as she sat down and she prayed that he couldn't tell that she'd been crying.

'That was Gina, Will's sister,' she told him.

Jake nodded, but he was frowning at Mattie and she wondered if he'd overheard her end of the conversation. What exactly had she said?

'Gina's my best friend,' she explained.

'Yes.' He was still frowning at her. 'I gathered that.'

What else had Jake 'gathered'? Why was he looking at her so ferociously? He couldn't possibly know about her surrogacy plans, could he? Somehow, Mattie just knew in her bones that he would be very upset if he discovered she was about to become pregnant with someone else's baby.

But it wasn't really any of his business, was it? He was going away for six months and by the time he came back he might have forgotten about her. He'd told her that he was footloose and fancy free and she was quite sure that was how he wanted to stay. Look at how easily he'd dumped Ange.

Just the same, his frown made Mattie nervous as she cut off a corner of toast and loaded it with egg. As she lifted the food to her mouth, Jake's hand shot across the table and he grabbed her wrist.

'Hey!' she cried as the food toppled back onto her plate. 'What was that for?'

'Aren't you allergic to eggs?'

'Oh.' She let out a whoosh of air. What a relief! His frowning concern had nothing to do with her phone conversation.

He pointed to her plate. 'The other morning when I made an omelette, you told me you were allergic to eggs.'

'You're right,' she admitted. 'Sorry. I'm afraid I was lying.'

Jake's relief was evident. 'I hope you had a good reason for lying.' He relaxed back in his chair and watched her with a look of dark bemusement.

'I had a very good reason. You were being mulish and I wanted to be mulish right back at you.'

'I was mulish?' He pretended to be shocked. 'When?'

Mattie thought about it and realised that her grounds for disliking Jake in those first couple of days had been based solely on the fact that he hadn't shown the slightest interest in her. It was an unsettling discovery and she certainly wasn't going to share it with him now.

'I…I can't remember the exact details,' she said lamely. She took another bite of egg and toast, but it seemed to stick in her throat. Suddenly she was thinking about everything that had happened since that morning Jake had made the omelette. How could she have undergone such a huge transformation in such a short space of time?

She hoped she didn't start crying again, but this morning she seemed to be faced by constant reminders of how deeply and swiftly she'd fallen for Jake. Heavens, from the moment she'd set eyes on him, she'd been sinking like a stone. And she'd promised herself this would never happen again!

She was still lost in thought when Jake glanced at his wristwatch and she was grateful for the distraction. 'It's almost time for you to leave for the airport.'

He sighed. 'I should book a taxi.'

'No, I'll drive you.'

'It's a long way and the traffic will be hell at this hour.'

Her eyes were threatening to water again. Damn. 'Jake, please don't argue. I'd like to take you to the airport.' Any time with him felt precious.

His throat made a swallowing motion and he looked almost as upset as she felt. 'Thanks, Mattie.' He picked up his breakfast things.

'Leave them.' Mattie was aghast by how brittle she sounded. 'I'll look after the kitchen. You go and get ready.'

'OK, OK.'

Her hands were shaking as she loaded the dishwasher, and she broke a cup. She'd just finished putting the pieces in the bin as Jake came in with a backpack swung over his shoulder.

She tried to sound relaxed. 'You travel light.'

He smiled crookedly. 'I'm not much of a shopper.'

'I'll just clean my teeth and get my bag.'

In a matter of moments she was back. Jake was holding Brutus and rubbing the little dog's silky ears. Brutus licked him under the chin. 'We're saying goodbye.'

Mattie nodded and bit her lip to hold back tears. 'I hope you said goodbye to Pavarotti too.'

'Oh, I did and he sang me an aria.'

She dug in her bag for her sunglasses and put them on before her eyes gave her away. 'I'll keep in touch with Roy for you.'

Jake smiled sadly. 'I don't suppose there's any point in trying to tell you that I don't expect you to worry about Roy.'

'No point at all. I'd love to visit him now and again.' Quickly, she went on, 'We'd better get going.'

'Yeah.'

She swung the strap of her bag over her shoulder and looked down at her car keys, took a deep breath.

'Mattie, are you OK?' Jake crossed the kitchen until he stood in front of her. He lifted her sunglasses and a soft groan broke from him when he saw her eyes filled with tears. With trembling hands, he framed her face.

She tried to smile and her mouth wobbled out of shape, but then it didn't matter because Jake was kissing her.

Mattie melted into his warm, strong embrace and she kissed him as if her life depended on it. And, afterwards, she felt a little reassured—a little calmer, which was just as well as she had to concentrate on driving in the heavy traffic.

By the time they reached Sydney's International Terminal her eyes were dry, her stomach reasonably composed. She hoped she could stay that way through the final farewell.

The airport was typically busy, with cars and taxis zapping in and out of parking spots, and travellers wheeling overloaded luggage trolleys onto pedestrian crossings.

'Just leave me here.' Jake pointed to a two-minute drop-off zone.

'Are you sure you don't want me to come in?'

He shook his head. 'It's going to take ages to get through security and you won't be able to come past the customs desk anyway. You know what it's like with international flights.'

'I hadn't thought about that. I've never been overseas.'
Jake's eyes widened. 'Really?'

'The furthest I've been is Western Australia.'

His eyebrows lifted in surprise. 'I guess you've been too busy looking after other people. You haven't had time to travel.'

'I guess.'

He smiled. 'It means you still have a lot of adventures ahead of you.'

Something about the way Jake said this made Mattie's heart leap like a flame. In a sudden burst of confidence, she asked, 'Do you have an e-mail address? It must be so lonely in Mongolia. I could write to you if you like.'

'Yeah, sure.' He pulled his wallet from his pocket and dug out a business card. 'Here you go.'

Mattie stared at his name, Jake R. Devlin, on the card and she felt her throat tighten. This small white rectangle was all she would have once Jake was gone, but she was so pleased that he wanted to stay in touch.

He extracted another card. 'You should write your e-mail address on the back of this one.'

'Of course.' She printed the address and handed him the card and he leaned in close, kissed her cheek.

Needing one last proper kiss, Mattie offered him her lips.

Car horns honked all around them and from somewhere above she could hear the roar of a plane taking off, but she wanted to take her own sweet time over this last lovely kiss.

Finally, Jake touched her cheek with a gentle caress of his fingertips. 'Take care, Mattie.'

'You too.'

He tapped the card she was holding. 'It'll be good to stay

in touch. I've had an amazing time.' Without warning, his face grew serious. His mouth hardened and turned down at the corners. 'But you do know that I can't promise you a future together, don't you?'

Mattie's heart clattered and bounced, as if it had fallen down a long flight of stairs. 'Of course,' she managed to say, but her voice was very tight and squeaky. 'I wasn't expecting a future with you.'

Even as the words left her lips, she knew they were a total lie, but Jake accepted them with a nod, then abruptly opened the car door. A second later, he was out on the footpath.

'I'll just grab my pack out of the back.' His voice was efficient and businesslike.

Mattie heard the slam of the car boot and then Jake was on the footpath once more, waving and smiling.

Smiling? How could he smile? A scant minute ago he'd taken all the joy out of her world. She lifted her hand to wave, tears blurring her vision.

Huge glass sliding doors opened behind him and he turned away from her and disappeared…

And Mattie's tears fell in earnest.

What a fool she'd been. She'd known from the start that Jake was dangerous and she'd tried so hard to resist him. But he was the most attractive man she'd ever met. North to her south.

Yesterday they'd had such a lovely morning together, but then, after the movie, she'd been stupid, stupid, stupid.

If only she hadn't been so weak. In less than twenty-four hours, she'd fallen completely in love.

With the wrong man.

Again.

* * *

Back at the flat, Mattie threw herself into a frenzied session of work and by the end of the day, she'd finished the painting that had given her trouble. This time, amazingly, the old magic was back. It was as if her creative energy was rushing to fill the despairing emptiness inside her.

When the painting was finished, she stood back, cuddling Brutus, and she examined the picture of Molly, the good little witch, silhouetted at her bedroom window, looking impossibly small and lonely.

Mattie was surprised by how poignant the picture seemed, and she smiled, satisfied with the effect. She really liked Molly's vulnerability and she knew her young readers would enjoy the secret knowledge that this skinny little girl was really a good witch, with super-powers that could help all the needy people in the houses below.

She only hoped she could find a similar strength in herself.

Jake sat in the mess hall at the mine site, lost in thought, wondering what Mattie was doing now. In his mind he could see her walking with Brutus along the path beside the bay, with the wind in her hair, her blue eyes sparkling.

He could see her working on a painting, her face serene yet completely focused. He could see her as she'd looked when she'd lain in bed beside him and he could remember the taste of her, the smell of her skin, the silky softness of her hair when he wound it around his fingers.

He could hear her musical voice, see the silver sparkle of her tears…

'Hey, Jake. There you are!'

Will Carruthers came through the doorway and helped himself to coffee, which he still preferred, even though most of the men drank the locally brewed Mongolian tea.

Will brought his mug to Jake's table and grinned at him. 'Good to see you, mate. How was your leave?'

'Not bad.' Jake was valiantly trying to shut down thoughts of Mattie.

Will's eyes narrowed. 'Do I detect a distinct lack of enthusiasm?'

'Sorry. I was miles away.'

'Dreaming about the hordes of beautiful women you left behind?' Will grinned again, but when Jake made no response he tried a different tack. 'Was everything in order at the flat?'

'Yes, absolutely.' Finally, Jake remembered his manners. 'Honestly, Will, thanks for letting me use your flat. It was fantastic. Terrific decor. Fabulous location. Oh, and I brought you a gift from the Duty Free. I'll drop it over to your *ger* tonight.'

Will grinned. 'Sounds like it's a bottle of my favourite refreshment.'

'More like three bottles,' Jake said, then he stared into the depths of his tea mug. He couldn't help it—he had to drag Mattie into the conversation. 'I suppose you know there was someone else staying at the flat.'

'Really? Who was it?'

'Mattie Carey.'

Will's eyes almost popped out of his head. 'Mattie was there at the same time as you?'

'She arrived a couple of days after me.'

'But I thought she wasn't due in Sydney until the fifth. Weren't you supposed to be gone by then? You said you were heading off to Japan to go skiing.'

Jake shook his head. 'Other way around. I went skiing first, and then I went to Sydney.'

'Oops.' Will smiled sheepishly. 'Sorry, I got that mixed

up.' He shot his friend a shrewd sideways glance. 'So how did it work out? Did you get on OK with Mattie?'

Jake was pleased that he managed to sound offhand. 'She was fine. She's an easy person to get along with.'

'Yeah, she would be.' Will chuckled. 'Good old Saint Matilda.'

Jake's flippancy vanished. 'Is that what you call her?'

'I meant it in the nicest possible way.' Will, watching Jake closely, back-pedalled fast. 'We all love Mattie. She's my sister's best friend, has been since forever. I think Gina and Mattie met in kindergarten.'

In the awkward silence that followed, Will sent Jake another sideways glance. 'I don't suppose Mattie mentioned why she's moved to Sydney?'

Jake shrugged. 'Not really. I thought she just wanted to work on her book.' He noticed the cautious tension in Will's face. 'Why do you ask? Was there another reason?'

Will shook his head, took a deep swig of coffee. When he lowered the mug, his face was as blank as a poker player's.

'So why did you ask if I knew anything?' Jake persisted.

'I was simply making conversation, man.'

Jake didn't believe him. He knew there was a chance that his perspective was skewed, but he was convinced now that Will knew something else about Mattie. A problem.

What could it be? Why else had she come to Sydney, other than to work on her book? Then again, why would she need to come to Sydney just to work on a children's story?

He thought back to when she'd first arrived. She'd said she had appointments.

A cold chill skittered down his spine. 'Mattie's not in Sydney to see doctors, is she? She's not ill?'

'No, mate. Keep your shirt on.' Will rolled his eyes, as if he was clearly convinced that his best mate had lost the plot. 'Mattie Carey is as healthy as a horse.'

'Then what did you mean? Why did you ask if I knew why she'd come to Sydney?'

'I've already forgotten. Chill, Jake. Forget I asked.' Will looked annoyed and he stood and snatched up his cup. 'The deal with the flat is nothing more than a friendly agreement. Mattie's renting it for twelve months and I'm very happy to have such a reliable tenant.'

Five days before the embryo transfer, Mattie began to receive progesterone injections. Trips to the clinic became part of her daily routine, along with working on her paintings and walking Brutus. She also borrowed several books about pregnancy from the library and began to conscientiously prepare super-healthy meals.

She bought a terracotta pot of parsley to grow on the balcony, so she had a ready source of iron. She wanted to do everything just right, even though she never thought of this baby as hers.

The embryo had already been created in a test tube from Gina and Tom's genetic material and Mattie saw herself as simply a glorified babysitter. Or perhaps a very fond aunt.

Whenever she felt slightly overawed by the task ahead, she focused on the fabulous and exciting moment in nine months' time when she handed a sweet little baby to her best friends.

It was a relief that things were finally happening and, as the date for the embryo transfer drew closer, Gina kept in e-mail contact almost every day. Neither she nor Mattie talked too much about the imminent pregnancy. Instead, they were just happy to keep in touch and to chat about Willowbank gossip, farming news, Mattie's progress on her new book…

Mattie quickly put a stop to any discussion about Jake and so far she hadn't replied to the e-mail he'd sent telling her about his journey and his first week settling back into life on the mine site.

Her reaction to it had been pure confusion. She was trying to 'get over' him and yet she'd been disappointed that he hadn't written straight away. Then she'd been disappointed by the matter-of-fact tone of his e-mail.

She wished she'd never suggested that they write. It would have been so much cleaner if they'd simply parted at the airport.

Whenever she thought about replying, she was frozen by uncertainty. She kept hearing those fateful words.

You do know that I can't promise you a future together, don't you?

She read the e-mail again and again, trying to search for hidden meanings. How crazy. Was she going to go through months of worrying about Jake the way she had with Pete? She couldn't face that again.

If she did decide to reply, it was hard to know what to say. She had to ask herself if it was right to behave as if her life was ticking along as usual, when the surrogacy was about to begin? She hated deceit of any kind.

However, there was a final reason she hadn't written to Jake, one she hardly dared to contemplate, that caught her out at unexpected moments, especially in the middle of the night.

As she lay in the dark, she found herself wondering if her intense feelings for him could pose a threat to the surrogacy. It was foolish to think this way when she knew they had no real future, but she couldn't help it. She'd never dreamed that the psychologist could be right and that she could meet someone like Jake before the baby was born.

And yet, here she was, wishing at times that she could keep her body for him.

But, in reality, if she was to have a man in her life at this point in time, she needed someone who would be there for her, no matter what—not a gorgeous, dangerous playboy.

She needed a man who was prepared to share her with the baby she carried, someone prepared to wait. Unfortunately, Jake Devlin couldn't tick a single box in her list of vital requirements and so she'd better just get over him, for her own sake.

Jake stared glumly at his computer screen. He'd downloaded his e-mails and again there was nothing from Mattie.

He looked at the back of the card, where she'd neatly printed her e-mail address, and for the hundredth time he remembered their farewell and her tears, and the passion in her last kiss. He could have sworn that she'd planned to write to him and he'd anticipated a constant stream of messages filled with typical Mattie-style warmth.

What did this silence mean?

What had changed?

His conversation with Will on his return kept haunting him. He kept hearing Will's harrowing question: *I don't suppose Mattie mentioned why she's moved to Sydney?*

Jake had quizzed his friend about it again, but Will always shrugged it off, claiming that Jake had misinterpreted a casual enquiry.

'What's got into you, mate?' Will had growled. 'Do you realise you grill me about Mattie Carey every time we meet? You need another holiday. You're way too tense.'

Perhaps Will was right. Jake knew he'd never been like this before. It was beyond crazy to be so uptight over a woman. He was usually trying to shake them off.

Ironically, as soon as he stopped expecting to hear from Mattie, an e-mail from her arrived in his in-box.

To: jakerdevlin@miningmail.com
From: mattiecarey@mymail.com
Hi Jake,
Greetings from sunny Sydney to deepest Mongolia.

I wanted to let you know that I brought Roy over here for morning tea today. We didn't make billy tea, but we had damper and lamingtons and I sent him home with a big bouquet of gum leaves and a vase so he can keep them in his room. As you can imagine, he was as happy as a possum in a hollow log.

Oh, and I found a book in a second-hand shop about old drovers and stockmen. It's full of photographs of the Outback and Roy loved it. He said to tell you he's well. Actually, he said he was fighting fit, but I think that's an exaggeration. And he sends his love.

I don't have much other news. I'm slowly knocking over the illustrations for the book and I'm afraid the coffee table never gets used as a coffee table any more.

I hope that French Canadian cook is feeding you well.

Are you still helping him out in the kitchen? Perhaps you should show him our recipe for pasta sauce?
Love from Brutus and Pavarotti,
Mattie xx

Jake was so relieved to hear from her that he swallowed his pride and wrote back straight away, but he kept the content deliberately light, just as she had. He told her about the party they'd had in the canteen for one of the team's birthday. And how they'd tried to play Scrabble last night in three different languages—English, French and Russian. He thanked her for taking care of Roy. He didn't mention a word about missing her.

Mattie replied the very next day and when he read her message he grinned. It was a single question:

What does the R in your name stand for? Robert? Roy? Rudolph? Rambo?

He wrote back that his middle name was Richard, named after his grandfather. And he asked about her middle name.

Mattie replied:

Middle name, Francesca, after my grandmother. Aren't we predictable?

After that, they exchanged e-mails almost every day. They kept their messages short, light and amusing, never hinting at anything like deeper emotions, and Jake was happy.

Mattie was pleased, too. After much deliberation, she'd decided finally to reply to Jake's e-mail. After all, maybe they could remain friends, just keep in touch? She wouldn't expect anything more.

It was best this way, Mattie decided, best that neither of them referred to that blissful night they'd spent in each other's arms again.

It made it easier for her to avoid telling Jake the truth.

Problem was, she still felt horribly guilty about that. And she was left with a helpless longing she didn't how to handle.

CHAPTER SIX

MATTIE was grinning as she dialled Gina's number.

'Guess what, girlfriend? It worked.'

'You mean—'

'I mean the tests came back positive.'

'Oh, my God! You mean we're pregnant?'

'Yep. We're pregnant. Very pregnant.'

Gina screamed in Mattie's ear. Then she began to gabble. 'I can't believe it's actually happening. Oh, God, you're so clever, Mattie. I'm crying. I don't know how to thank you.'

'I'm excited too. I'm so glad it's really on the way. There's going to be a baby.'

'How do you feel?'

'OK. Relieved. I've been fairly sure for the last few days, but the doctor didn't want me to say anything to you until he was certain.'

'So do you have symptoms? Can you tell me all about it?'

Patiently, Mattie told her best friend everything, how her breasts had become increasingly tender and she'd been feeling dreadfully tired. At first she'd been worried she was coming down with something, but then she'd started losing her breakfast and she *knew*.

'Oh, Mattie, I still can't take it in. I'm just so excited, but you poor thing. Is it too awful?'

'It's only yuck for about an hour a day. Most of the time, I feel pretty good. And I have the perfect excuse to take a daytime nap. The really good news is, the doctor's very happy. He said the hormone levels are really strong. Like *really* strong.'

'I see.' Gina's voice grew cautious. 'That sounds like it means something.'

'Well, yes. It's nothing to panic about…but…um… there might be more than one baby.'

Gina screamed again. 'Oh, my gosh—*two*! Do you mind if I hang up? I've got to go and find Tom.'

Mattie laughed. 'Off you go. Give Tom my love.'

When she hung up the phone, she sank onto the sofa. Brutus jumped up beside her and she let him snuggle close.

'Two babies, Brutus,' she whispered. 'I'm going to end up the size of a house.'

With her hand resting on her still flat tummy, she tried to imagine it filled with two lively full-term babies. Twins were a risk, the doctor had warned her when he'd transferred two embryos, but at the time she'd been happy to take the chance. One way or another, she'd wanted Gina and Tom to have a family.

But yikes. How would her figure ever recover? She couldn't help wondering what Jake would think if he saw her, swollen and huge, but then she quickly dismissed that question.

Jake had only entered her life for a few short days and this was something that had been decided months ago. It was a private matter between herself and her oldest and dearest friends. Jake had no part in this.

If only that realisation didn't make her feel so desperately lonely and sad.

I'm being selfish...

She tried to remind herself that she'd been perfectly happy before she'd met Jake. And now her focus had to be positive. She had to concentrate on the wonderful gift she was carrying.

It was an amazing privilege to be able to do this for Gina and Tom. They were going to be fabulous parents and she was going to help them have the perfect little family they so thoroughly deserved.

Gina and Tom's babies would have a happy and idyllic childhood on the farm, going to school in Willowbank, making friends with the local children.

A new generation.

Mattie had such happy memories of her own schooldays with Gina and Tom and Will and Lucy. It was too long since the old 'gang' had been together. Perhaps there would be a gathering for the babies' christening?

What fun!

And what about Jake?

Wouldn't it be wonderful if he could fit into that picture?

As always, when Mattie thought about Jake, she felt a painful jolt in the centre of her chest. There'd been no recent e-mails because he was away in the wilds of Mongolia on some kind of expedition, and she was shocked by how much she missed him. But she knew it was foolish to feel so attached when he'd told her in no uncertain terms that he didn't fit into her future. She'd spent a couple of days with him and now they exchanged brief, chatty e-mails—it had been impossible to cut Jake off altogether. But it was barely the beginnings of a relationship.

Even so, she found it ridiculously easy to imagine Jake being absorbed into her circle of friends. He was already good friends with Will. And Mattie knew he would like her other friends and they would like him. She could picture them all sitting around a dinner table—at Gina and Tom's perhaps.

In her imagination, she could picture it all—driving down to Willow Creek Farm with Jake, bringing wine and cheese from her favourite boutique deli, and arriving via the winding road that led through a grove of pines to Gina and Tom's farmhouse.

They would be welcomed by Tom, wearing the black and white apron he always donned when he was helping in the kitchen. Jake, with his handsome looks and flashing dark eyes, would be a huge hit with the girls and the men would like his laid-back humour. Around the table, they would share stories and lots of laughter along with scrumptious food.

Yes, Jake would fit in very well. How perfect it could be. *But it's impossible and I'm a fool to even think of it.*

To: mattiecarey@mymail.com
From: jakerdevlin@miningmail.com
Hey there, Mattie.
I'm back at last after spending three weeks out in the wild wastes of Mongolia on a prospecting expedition. Won't bore you with details, but it's very acceptable to be back in a properly built ger with a comfortable bed and a fire at night.

Hope all's well. Would you believe I miss you and Brutus and Pavarotti and your drawings of Molly?

How are you? A man needs details. How are you spending your days? What colour is your hair now? What movies have you seen?

More importantly, what colour are you wearing under your T-shirt?
Keep smiling,
Jake xx

Mattie read this and burst into tears.

She'd had a shocker of a day. A headache had started mid-morning and, because she was pregnant and couldn't take tablets, there was nothing she could do but lie down with a cool cloth on her forehead. She'd sprinkled the cloth with drops of lavender oil, but now she was sick of the smell of lavender and her headache hadn't budged.

Her waist was expanding exponentially. She felt fat and ugly and tired and miserable...and Jake was fantasising about her in sexy underwear. It was too much!

She let out a moan of pure self-pity and Brutus whimpered and looked up at her with eyes filled with concern.

'Oh, Brutus,' she sobbed, scooping him up for a cuddle. 'What am I going to do about Jake?'

She knew for absolute certain now that she was carrying twins. She'd seen the ultrasound images and there they were—two little heads, two sets of arms and legs, swimming in their own little sacs. So cute! But already she'd had to buy maternity jeans and her breasts were so heavy now she'd had to buy maternity bras—horrid, hefty harnesses, only available in white, black or beige that made her feel like an ageing matron.

Meanwhile, Jake thought he was writing to a slim young woman who wore sexy lace and satin lingerie in a range of rainbow colours, a woman who had no commitments other than her writing deadlines.

She was a fraud, an impostor, a cheat!

With a helpless sigh, she set Brutus down and began to pace the floor, the little dog at her heels. What should she do? Should she reply? How *could* she reply honestly?

Oh, help. She couldn't keep stringing Jake along like this. But should she simply drop the communication and let him assume that she'd lost interest?

She didn't want to let him go.

I have to.

Tears fell again and she snatched up tissues and mopped her face. If only she didn't have this headache, she could think more clearly. She went through to the kitchen and made a cup of camomile tea, which she took through to the lounge room. Curled on the sofa, she sipped the herbal brew and tried to think calmly.

OK. First, she was pregnant but she couldn't tell Jake what was happening to her.

Why?

It's a private matter and, anyway, he's not serious about me. He's already warned me there's no chance of forever.

But couldn't he change his mind? He seemed really keen when he was in Sydney.

Even if he was keen, the pregnancy would douse his passion in a heartbeat. He's a playboy. A woman pregnant with someone else's babies would send him running for the hills.

Too true. Mattie had enough emotional issues just coping with the surrogacy, without letting Jake mess with her head. He would never understand why she was doing this.

Bottom line, she didn't want to be helplessly and miserably in love again. She didn't want to feel vulnerable and endlessly anxious, the way she had with Pete.

After all, how could she expect to share this surrogacy

with a guy who'd openly claimed he had an allergy to commitment?

Heavens, why did she even hesitate when she had so many clear answers? Any way she looked at this, she only had one sensible option.

She should stop writing to Jake…let him go…

It was the only decent thing to do. And, given how easily he'd parted from his previous girlfriend, he probably wouldn't be upset.

No doubt thousands of e-mail exchanges ended when one person fell silent.

No doubt the world was filled with thousands of broken hearts.

Jake switched off his computer, poured himself a measure of vodka and downed it in one fiery gulp. He poured another and downed it too, went to the small window and stared out at the other *gers* scattered over the barren ground. He saw lights burning in most of the tents but he wasn't in the mood for company.

That in itself wasn't surprising. He'd always been a loner, a self-sufficient outsider, who'd learned as a child to get along without company. But there was a difference between being alone and being lonely.

Tonight, as he looked out into the desert night, he could feel the almost forgotten loneliness of his child-hood creeping back, sneaking beneath his defences. He was remembering again the long lonesome months after his mother's breakdown, when she wouldn't—couldn't speak to him.

He flinched at the memory, working hard to dismiss the pain of her bewildering rejection. He'd adored his mother but he'd learned even then, at the age of nine, that he could drown beneath the weight of such love.

More than one girlfriend had accused him of emotional bankruptcy, and he knew he'd deserved the accusation, but he'd learned the hard way to keep his heart safely under lock and key.

This was precisely why he'd told Mattie that he couldn't offer any promises for the future.

So it didn't make any kind of sense that his old anxieties were staging a comeback now, simply because he hadn't heard from her in over a month.

He'd sent her three more e-mails and she hadn't replied. He couldn't believe how much he needed to hear from her, needed to know she was OK.

Will Carruthers could shed no light on her silence and in the end Jake knew there was only one thing to do. He had to ring the Sydney flat, had to hear her voice, to know at least that she wasn't ill.

As he dialled through the international codes, then added the flat's telephone number, he was ridiculously nervous—so damn nervous he was sweating. His hands were clammy and he felt sick, like a teenager trying to pluck up the courage to ask a girl on a first date.

When Mattie answered the phone his throat was dry and his voice as rough as gravel. 'Hello, Mattie.'

'Is that Jake?'

'Yes. How are you?'

'Are you still in Mongolia?'

She sounded shocked and scared. Why did she sound so unhappy?

'Yes, I'm still here.' What could he say now? The light banter of e-mails became downright stupid when said out loud. 'I haven't heard from you for a while, so I thought I'd check in. How are you? Everything OK?'

'Yes, fine.' Her voice sounded anything but fine. 'I…I've been really busy.'

Jake gritted his teeth. How the hell had he thought this call was a good idea?

What now? On the basis of one night of passion, he could hardly demand an explanation for Mattie's silence.

'How are you?' he asked again and he sounded way too tense. 'Are you well?'

'I'm really well, Jake.'

'You sound a bit…' He paused, searching for the right word.

'I'm a bit tired, that's all. I…I've taken on some extra work and it…it's keeping me really busy.'

'So are you enjoying this work? Is it creative?'

He thought he heard a definite sigh.

'Yes, Jake, it's highly creative.'

This time, there was no mistaking her tone. It was most definitely let's-drop-this-subject.

Jake wished he could see her. If he could look into her eyes, he might be able to see what she wasn't telling him. He would know whether she was happy.

'I've been in touch with Roy,' she said. 'I…I haven't had time to visit him lately, but I ring him every week. He's keeping well.'

'That's good to hear. Thanks for keeping an eye on him.'

'How's Will?' she asked carefully.

'Oh, he's fighting fit. Actually, he's on leave at the moment in California. He should be having a great time.'

'Sounds like fun. Are you going somewhere like that for your next leave?'

Jake's stomach hit the floor. This was a brush-off with no holds barred. Mattie was letting him know that she clearly didn't expect to see him.

OK, so maybe he had dropped a strong warning when he'd farewelled her at the airport, but he felt differently now. He'd missed her. Maybe he'd even changed. He certainly wasn't going to give in easily.

Swallowing his pride, he said, 'I was wondering what would happen if I turned up on your doorstep.'

This was met by silence.

Jake held his breath, couldn't believe how bad he felt.

'I…I…' Mattie was obviously flustered. 'Are you planning to come back here?'

Somehow, he forced himself to ask, 'Will you still be there in a month or two?'

Another awkward silence chilled him to the bone. And then, 'Jake, I'm afraid I'm going to be really busy for the next few months.'

Really busy… He bit back a swear word. Felt sick. This was the ultimate rebuff.

'You mean you'd rather not see me?'

'It'll be difficult.' It was barely more than a whisper and yet he heard the break in her voice.

Why? What was going on? He remembered Mattie's tears when they'd said goodbye. He'd been egotistical enough to think they'd meant she was going to miss him, but was there another reason? Something she wasn't telling him?

One thing was certain. This phone call wasn't giving him any answers and there was no point in prolonging the torture. 'OK. Thanks for setting me straight on that,' he said, battling disbelief that he could actually let her go like this…without a fight.

'Goodbye, Jake.'

He heard a click on the end of the line and, just like that, Mattie Carey was out of his life.

But Jake was left with a niggling doubt, a gut awareness that she hadn't really wanted to let him go.

Or was that simply his ego getting in the way of common sense?

In a harbourside café, Gina sipped a coffee latte with a dreamy smile. She sighed happily as she set it down. 'How lucky are we to have a boy and a girl? It's so perfect. I can't believe it. I keep wanting to cry with happiness.'

Mattie grinned and slipped her arm around her friend's shoulders. Having her friends with her for the ultrasound this morning had made such a difference. Seeing the joy on their faces and treasuring the warmth of their hugs had made everything about this project totally worthwhile.

She could forget about the headaches, the heartburn and the tiredness. If she held in her mind this picture of her friends' happy, smiling faces and the cute black and white images of their two little babies, she could blank out memories of Jake Devlin.

She had done the right thing when she'd ended the phone call. It was the only sane way to approach this, wasn't it? After all, if her fiancé hadn't been able to stay in love with her when she'd been younger and prettier and *not* pregnant, how could she possibly expect a rake like Jake to stay interested in her now?

It was a cold, blustery winter's day when Jake returned to Sydney. He stepped out of the taxi and gusts of wind whipped at him. Sharp rain needled his face. Not exactly a warm welcome, but then he hadn't expected one.

On the overnight flight he hadn't slept, but when he checked in to his hotel he went straight to his room, showered and changed and then hurried downstairs again to collect the hire car he'd booked. Rain lashed at the windscreen as he drove out of the hotel car park and joined the steady stream of traffic.

For a fleeting moment he felt strangely disoriented. The busy arterial road in the frantic heart of Sydney was such a bizarre contrast to the moonscape world of the remote mine site he'd so recently left. He blinked to clear his head, changed lanes and took a right turn at the next set of lights. He'd planned to head straight to Roy's nursing home but now he realised too late he was going the wrong way.

He continued on, looking for a suitable place to make a U-turn, and he recognised the camping store where Mattie had bought the little gas ring and billy can for Roy's tea party.

This direction led to Will's flat.

To Mattie.

Knots tightened in his gut and his heart began to thud.

OK, OK. If he was already heading this way, he might as well drive past the flat. And if he saw Mattie's car parked in the drive, he might as well go in. Get it over and done with. He had to see her at least once. Maybe he was fooling himself that she hadn't really wanted to let him go, but he had to know the truth. Had to sort this out, face to face.

In that disastrous phone call, Mattie had mentioned that she was so busy she'd begun telephoning Roy rather than visiting him. That had surprised Jake and he couldn't help worrying that there was a problem. Why would the same girl who'd gone above and beyond in her efforts to please Roy suddenly be too busy to pay him an occasional visit?

He still couldn't shake the feeling that she was in some kind of trouble. At the risk of totally annoying her, he couldn't let her go until he got to the bottom of this mystery.

Mattie was working near a window in the lounge room, listening to the rhythm of the rain as she drew a preliminary sketch for another illustration.

The book was almost finished and she wanted to have everything off to her publisher in the next few weeks—before the last weeks of the pregnancy drained her energy.

She was concentrating hard, trying to capture exactly the right level of simmering excitement in Molly's facial expression, when a sound from the street outside caught her attention. She glanced through the window and saw a sleek, low black car shooting a spray of water from the gutter as it pulled up in front of the flats.

She wasn't expecting anyone, so she paid the car a cursory glance and went back to her drawing. But then the car door slammed and Brutus began to yap.

'Quiet, Brutus!' Mattie glanced outside again, frowning. Her little dog only yapped to welcome people he knew and liked. Strangers were greeted by silence, or by a low, mean-spirited growl.

Curious now, she watched a man make a dash through the sheeting rain. He was wearing a black waterproof jacket and blue jeans and she admired his considerable height, his thick dark hair and broad shoulders.

Oh, God. Oh, help.

No!

It couldn't be Jake.

Her heart stopped beating altogether. The pencil fell from her nerveless fingers and clattered to the table, then her heart gave one terrified bound and began to hammer again. Painfully.

Jake.

It was Jake.

Too shocked to move, she sat and watched as he flipped the latch on the front gate and dashed up the path, head down against the rain.

She hadn't heard from him since that dreadful phone call. She hadn't expected him to come, had *never dreamed* he would come.

Instinctively, she wrapped her arms over her ballooning stomach. One of the babies kicked, and then the other joined in. A kicking competition began.

Jake knocked on the door and Brutus darted forward, yapping excitedly. Mattie tried to stand, but her knees shook and her legs refused to support her. What would Jake think when he saw her?

He knocked again.

CHAPTER SEVEN

JAKE knew for certain that Mattie was home. Not only was her car in the garage, he'd caught a glimpse of her worried face at the window. But now she wasn't answering his knock.

Terrific. He wasn't welcome.

Stubbornly, he knocked again.

Her little dog yapped madly and scratched on the other side of the door. At least Brutus was happy to see him.

The Mediterranean-blue door remained firmly shut.

He shouldn't have come.

Acid rose in his stomach. After Mattie's clear rejection, coming here was close to the stupidest thing he'd ever done.

Teeth gritted, hands clenched, he turned his back on the flat and scowled at the driving rain. No way would he knock on that door a third time. A man had his pride.

Which meant he had no choice but to get out of here and bid Mattie Carey good riddance. He didn't need this kind of angst in his life, couldn't believe he'd allowed himself to become entangled in this mess.

He turned, ready to make a dash for the car, when the door opened behind him and Brutus leapt out, yapping madly and jumping at Jake's knees in an ecstasy of welcome.

'Sit, Brutus. Down, boy.'

Mattie's voice. Jake looked up and there she stood in the doorway.

Thud.

Her light brown hair was a soft cloud about her pale face and her blue eyes were huge and worried. She ordered Brutus to settle and she bent to pat the dog, then straightened again. She was wearing a voluminous cherry-red tunic over dark grey leggings and black ankle boots. She was the Mattie he remembered.

Even lovelier than he remembered. She had a special glow about her.

She was…

Jake went cold all over.

No.

No way. She couldn't be.

'Hello, Jake.'

He couldn't drag his eyes from the unmistakable curve of her stomach.

No way. *No!*

During her silence, he'd considered many possibilities. Never this.

What did it mean? Was he going to be a father?

The thought sent blood pounding through him. Dazed, he gestured in the direction of her middle.

'Why?' He gulped, couldn't get the question out. Tried again. 'Why didn't you tell me?'

She shook her head. 'I couldn't. I'm so sorry.'

Couldn't? What the hell did that mean? 'What's going on, Mattie? Why couldn't you have said something?'

She pressed shaking fingers against her lips, looked ready to cry.

'You haven't got a husband lurking in the wings?'

'No, of course not.'

'You are pregnant, aren't you? It's not...something else?'

'I'm fine,' she said, but she looked anything but fine. 'I'm really well. And yes...I'm pregnant.'

'OK. Right.' Jake raised a hand to loosen his tie, realised he wasn't wearing one. 'On to the next question then... Is it mine?'

The sudden eagerness in his voice shocked him. He hadn't planned on fatherhood, had always made certain that he'd avoided any chance of unplanned offspring. But everyone knew these accidents happened. And Mattie would be the world's best mother. And somehow the idea of her—

Again, she shook her head. 'Don't panic, Jake. You're not about to become a father.'

Not the father.

She might as easily have landed a king hit on Jake's jaw. The result would have been the same.

She had another lover.

He was stunned. Flattened. Shocked by how disappointed he felt.

He dragged in a ragged breath, let it out through clenched teeth and jerked his gaze from the dismay in her eyes to the glistening wet concrete on the driveway.

A thousand questions rained on him. If the baby wasn't his, who the hell's was it? When had this happened? Before he'd met Mattie? Afterwards?

Hell.

Could he believe anything she told him? Short of a DNA test, how could he be certain that the child was his or was not his?

He shot a searching glance at Mattie and high colour rose in her cheeks.

Without quite meeting his gaze, she said, 'This is a surprise.'

'Of course it is.'

'I mean, I wasn't expecting to see you.'

'I dare say.' He couldn't hold back the bitterness from his voice.

Her hand fluttered protectively over her middle. 'I know this is a shock, Jake. I'm sorry.' A small huffing sigh escaped. 'It's complicated.'

'How complicated?'

'Quite.' She chewed her lip. 'Very complicated, actually.'

Before he could snap a biting retort, the bright colour in Mattie's face faded, leaving a gravity that disturbed him. She took a step back.

'You'd better come in. You deserve an explanation.'

When he didn't move immediately, she said again, 'Please, Jake, come inside.'

Until now, he hadn't realised that he'd been secretly hoping to spend his leave with this woman. What a mistake. Jake-the-Rake Devlin never spent his leave with the same girl he'd been with on the last leave.

Right now he should have been partying in Paris or skiing in the Snowy Mountains.

But here he was, back in the flat with Mattie. A sinking sense of foreboding chilled him to the bone as he shrugged out of his coat and hung it on a peg by the door, then followed Mattie into the familiar lounge room. Will's lounge room.

Jake almost staggered under the weight of another alarming possibility. *No, please, no. Don't let the baby be Will's.*

It wasn't possible, was it? But Will had been so cagey about Mattie…and she was living in his flat…

But surely they would have told him? A wave of panicky loneliness swept over him, the frightening sensation of loss that he remembered from his childhood.

He shook it off and reined in his galloping thoughts.

'Take a seat, Jake.'

Mattie pointed to one of the leather sofas that faced each other on either side of the glass coffee table. He saw that she'd set a card table by the window and had covered it with her art paraphernalia. He remembered how she'd once sat cross-legged on the floor while she drew the illustrations for her children's book. No doubt her burgeoning figure made that impossible now.

'Would you like tea or coffee?' she asked.

He shook his head. *Just the truth.*

With a worried little sigh, she sat opposite him.

Opposite. Not cosily next to him, as the Mattie of old would have done.

She looked down at her hands and he followed her gaze, saw that her fingernails had been painted a deep, glamorous red to match her top. The strong colour made her pale hands look elegant and sophisticated. Even lovelier than before.

A handful of pebbles lodged in Jake's throat and he manfully swallowed every one of them.

'I'm really sorry you've found out like this,' she said. 'It's the last thing I wanted. I know it's a shock.'

Biting back the barrage of questions he longed to fire at her, he cracked a bitter smile and very deliberately relaxed back into the soft leather upholstery, legs casually crossed at the ankles.

Mattie watched him and thought how utterly wonderful he looked. If she wasn't so nervous and anxious she would have been deliriously happy. How fantastic it would be to do nothing more than to sit here and feast her eyes on Jake Devlin.

Oh…it was *so* good to see him again.

He was wearing a cream cable-knit sweater and blue denim jeans. A five o'clock shadow darkened his jaw and his hair had been ruffled by the rain and wind, reminding her of the dangerously handsome pirate she'd met on the first day she'd arrived at this flat.

She wished she could throw herself across the room and curl up beside him. She longed to feel his arms about her, to rest her head on his shoulder and to feel the soft bulky wool of his sweater against her cheek. She needed to bury her face in his neck and smell his skin, longed to feel his sexy lips on hers.

Heavens, maybe pregnancy hormones had caused a spike in her libido, but she wanted nothing more than to rip off his lovely sweater and run her hands all over his gorgeous body. Wanted him to want her the way he'd wanted her last time.

But she'd relinquished such privileges. And now Jake looked hard and distanced. The short gap across the coffee table was as vast as the Grand Canyon.

Jake stretched an arm along the back of the sofa and his dark eyes rested on her pregnant tummy. 'So this is why you've been so busy? This is your new creative project?'

With nervous fingers, Mattie smoothed the hem of her tunic over her leggings. 'To be honest, I've actually been more tired than busy.'

'It's rather late for honesty, Mattie.'

'Yes,' she admitted softly.

'You've kept your condition a state secret. Why?'

'I didn't have much choice, Jake. I wanted to tell you, but I'd promised that I wouldn't tell anyone.'

Before he could open his mouth to fire another question, Mattie hurried on. 'I suppose I could have asked for permission to tell you, but I was worried that, even if I did *try* to explain, you still wouldn't understand.'

'I have an honours degree in biological science. I do have a reasonable understanding of how these things happen.'

Ignoring his sarcasm, she tried again. 'This is a particularly delicate situation.'

To her surprise, Jake's skin turned pale despite his tan. 'Please tell me the baby's not Will's.'

'Will's?' Mattie almost choked on her shock. 'Good heavens, no. How could you think that?'

'From where I'm sitting, anything's possible.' As his colour returned, he said, 'I presume all this secrecy is to hide the father's identity?'

She nodded. 'And the mother's.'

'I beg your pardon?'

She patted the firm mound of her stomach. 'This is a surrogate pregnancy.'

Jake's brow creased. His mouth opened and shut, but he didn't speak. He said nothing to reassure Mattie, or to help her through this awkward disclosure.

When the silence became unbearable, she drew a deep breath and dived in. 'My best friend Gina—Will's sister—had a condition called endometriosis and it was so bad that the doctors more or less ordered her to have a hysterectomy. It was just awful for her. She was only thirty, and she and her husband, Tom, who's the loveliest guy, were planning a big family.'

'They could have adopted,' Jake commented dryly.

'Yes, they certainly considered adoption.'

He shot her a withering glance. 'But you had a better idea.'

Mattie let out a gloomy sigh. This was exactly the reaction she'd expected from Jake. He wasn't going to spare her a moment's sympathy or understanding. She lifted her gaze to the ceiling as she searched for the right words.

'I think this is a much better option. It means Gina and Tom can have their own children. The doctors were able to use Gina's eggs and Tom's sperm to grow the embryos.'

'So now *their* baby is growing in *your* body?'

There was no avoiding the clear disapproval in his voice.

'That's right.'

Across the room, their gazes locked. Mattie saw the shocked light in Jake's eyes. He could never understand. He believed she was crazy.

But it was no comfort to realise she'd been right when she'd anticipated this kind of reaction. It was no comfort now to know she should never have become involved with him. No comfort to face the truth that she'd been weak at the one point in her life when she'd needed to be really strong.

Almost wearily, Jake asked, 'So, when did this happen?'

'After you went back to Mongolia.'

'But I suppose you already had the surrogacy planned? You knew on the night you slept with me that you were going to go ahead with this?'

'Yes.' Mattie's chin lifted. 'But I don't see why you're on your high horse, Jake. This pregnancy isn't any of your business.'

'Really?' he asked coldly.

'You know you never planned a future with me.'

His face was suddenly stern and as hard as granite.

'You can't have it both ways, Jake. You can't carry on like a playboy and then disapprove because I want to give my friends the wonderful gift of two babies.'

This time his mouth stayed open rather a long time. '*Two* babies?' he repeated faintly.

'Yes. Twins. A boy and a girl.'

The news sent him lurching to his feet. His throat worked as he stared again at her stomach. He dragged tense fingers through his hair. 'How could you do this to yourself, Mattie?'

'I've already told you. I wanted to help Gina and Tom.'

'Oh, yes, of course. I should have known.' His smile was falsely bright. 'Saint Matilda.'

The words hit her like a slap. 'You've been talking to Will.'

Jake shrugged.

'You have, haven't you? You've been talking to Will Carruthers about me.'

'I had to tell him that we'd met. After all, we were sharing his flat.'

'And he told you he called me Saint Matilda?'

'Appropriately, as it turns out.'

Jake turned his back on her and stared through the window at the rain, hands thrust in pockets, jaw at a stubborn angle, while Mattie smarted. Had Will suggested that she was crazy too? Surely not. He was Gina's brother.

'I knew you would never understand,' she said miserably to Jake's back.

'And you were dead right.' He whipped around to face her. 'I don't understand. I *really* don't understand.'

He began to pace the room, turned abruptly to face her. 'Hell, Mattie, I know you like to help people. You make a habit of going out of your way to help just about everyone you meet and that's fine, but you've taken it too far this time. You're young and single. You should be making the most of your youth. Having fun. You've never been overseas. Why not try that instead of turning yourself into a damned incubator? That's crazy.'

An incubator!

'How dare you call me that?' Squaring her shoulders, Mattie fought to defend herself. 'If you knew Gina and Tom, you wouldn't call me crazy.'

He dismissed this with a shrug and she felt anger rise through her like steam. Righteous anger. This reaction was exactly what she'd expected and feared. It was why she'd remained silent, why she'd told him not to come.

Nevertheless, she was hurt. Why couldn't he understand?

'This was my decision, Jake. It's my body. My business. I'm perfectly healthy and I'm in no danger. I don't need your permission. Besides, you were on the other side of the world.' She dropped her gaze to her hands, clenched tightly in her lap. 'You know you were never planning to be a part of my life.'

She sensed rather than saw the way his entire body stiffened, but when she lifted her gaze she saw something else in his expression that made her heart stand still.

Oh, heavens. What was it?

Fear? Confusion and disappointment? Tenderness? All of these things?

His distress shocked her. She hadn't expected this. Jake was a renowned ladies' man. She'd seen for herself how quickly he'd lost interest in his previous girlfriend. He'd warned Mattie off at their final parting.

Now her throat ached with welling tears as she watched him standing there, shoulders slumped, hands sunk in pockets, throat working as he stared morosely at her drawing of Molly.

Had she been wrong?

Did Jake actually care?

What should she do? What *could* she do or say? Was it too late? How could she find the courage to take the vital step that might bridge the gap between them? She wasn't even sure it was possible now.

Should she tell him that the night she'd slept with him had been the most moving and beautiful night of her life? Should she admit how hard it had been to give him up?

She wondered if she could tell Jake the other truth, the one she'd barely admitted, even to herself. That she'd been scared that her strong feelings for him might have prevented her from going ahead with the surrogacy.

Watching him, Mattie was gripped by a terrible confusion. For the first time in her life, her vision of right and wrong was unclear. Until now, doing the right thing had always felt safe and reassuring, but now doubts flooded her.

She watched his stiff back and his hard, grim profile and she longed to go to him, to reach out, to throw her arms around him and to tell him how utterly gorgeous he was. But could she be sure that he wanted that?

She was still struggling to find the right answer when Jake turned slowly.

His face was cold. 'I'm pleased I called in,' he said icily. 'At least the truth is out now.'

She'd handled this badly. So badly. 'I'm sorry,' she said, but those two words had never sounded so inadequate.

Jake shook his head. 'It's too late to be sorry. It's…it's simply too late.' He began to cross the room, heading for the door.

Mattie stood quickly, and she flinched as one of the babies kicked hard in protest. 'Do you have to go already?'

'Of course. As you put it so clearly—I'm not exactly a part of your life.'

Brutus started to whimper at Jake's feet and he bent down to pat the dog and gave him a scratch between his ears. Mattie wished that she could whimper too. Perhaps, if she cried, Jake would give her a scratch behind the ears. A pat? Any tiny sign?

Get a grip, girl.

He was already opening the front door.

Desperately grasping at straws, she stammered, 'I…I haven't t-told you about Roy. And…and you haven't told me about Mongolia.'

'Give me a break, Mattie. You aren't remotely interested in Mongolia.'

'That's not true. Anyway, wouldn't you like to hear about Roy?'

'I can visit Roy and get the news straight from the horse's mouth.' He pushed the door wider.

She would never see him again.

Her legs almost caved beneath her. She took a shaky step towards the door. 'You're really upset. You're angry, aren't you?'

Jake didn't reply. Without another word, he stepped outside and closed the door quietly but firmly behind him.

She'd lost him.

Mattie collapsed in a shaking huddle on the sofa, unable to stop her tears. She went through almost a whole box of tissues, but no amount of crying could ease the terrible ache inside her.

It had been so dreadfully hard to see Jake again, reminding her of everything she'd given up.

She'd never had a boyfriend like Jake Devlin, might never meet anyone like him ever again.

And now she'd lost him.

She'd watched that door close behind him and it had felt like a death—more than Mattie could bear—and it was ages before she could think clearly, before she could chastise herself for breaking her heart over another man.

It wasn't as if Jake's departure was anything like the break-up with Pete. She and Jake hadn't been engaged. Not even close. There'd been no *understanding*. Jake hadn't promised forever. He'd never pretended to be anything but a footloose and fancy free bachelor.

Heavens, she shouldn't even be crying over him. If she was going to shed any tears over Jake Devlin, they should be tears of anger.

Heck, yes. As Mattie grabbed another handful of tissues, she deliberately stopped feeling sorry for herself and focused instead on all the reasons she should be angry with Jake. There were so many!

First, he had no right to storm in here and throw a tantrum simply because she wasn't available for another holiday fling. Second, he had no right to criticise her when she was doing something wonderful for Gina and Tom.

Third, it was impossible for him to understand why she'd made this choice because he was so jolly self-centred. And, most hurtful of all—he'd refused to show her an ounce of the compassion he'd showered on his old friend, Roy.

All in all, Jake was an opinionated and selfish prig and she was better off without him.

But…heaven help her, he was gorgeous too. She adored everything about the man—his flashing dark eyes, his cheeky smile, his happy laugh, his electrifying caresses, his sensational kisses…

Oh, good grief, she was hopeless.

Why couldn't he have stayed in Mongolia?

Jake tossed his coat onto the back seat of the hire car and slammed the door. Letting fly with a string of expletives, he wrenched open the driver's door, slid behind the steering wheel and pulled that door shut with an even louder slam.

He gunned the engine and took off, charging down the street at a reckless speed—until he saw the shocked face of a pedestrian and rapidly slowed down, chastened.

As soon as he turned the corner out of Mattie's street, he saw a parking space and pulled into it. His breathing was still ragged, his heart still pounding. He couldn't remember the last time he'd felt this angry. Or this scared.

Actually, that was a lie.

Jake remembered all too well.

He knew exactly when he'd felt this way and the very thought of it drenched him in a cold sweat, but it was too late to stop the memories of that terrible night when his baby brother had been born.

He'd been nine years old and thrilled, because after years of nagging his parents they'd told him that at last he was going to have a baby brother or sister.

He'd been caught up in a whirlwind of excitement during the preparations for the baby's arrival—painting the little back bedroom, watching parcels of impossibly cute clothes arrive from city stores, seeing nursery furniture coming out of storage.

Jake had made a rattle for the baby, a pathetic thing

really, but at the time he'd been so proud, filling a small plastic bottle with seeds and painting it rainbow colours.

He'd imagined the baby playing with it, laughing and bashing it on the floor, and he'd dreamed of a future when the baby could crawl and the two of them would play hide and seek together.

He had such plans—so many things he would teach the youngster—how to swim and to ride, how to climb trees, catch a ball, keep secrets from grown-ups.

But then that night had come.

His father and Roy had been away mustering and Jake and his mother had been alone in the homestead. In the middle of the night Jake had been woken by the sound of his mother's raised voice. He'd crept out of bed to find her, with her dressing gown clutched about her, crying into the telephone, begging the flying doctor to come.

Terror had struck Jake's heart. His mother had looked so white and ill, so frightening, with tears streaming down her face. She had been shaking, but when she'd put the phone down she'd brushed his worried questions aside and hurried straight to the two-way radio to call his father.

The men had been asleep and it was ages before anyone answered. His mother had broken down while she'd waited and, when she'd finally managed to speak, her words had been obscured by her sobbing.

Jake had hated to see her like this. He'd tried to hug her, demanding to know what had happened.

At last she'd stopped crying and she'd touched his cheek with a cold hand. 'I need you to be a brave, good boy, Jake. The flying doctor's coming. Can you turn on all the house lights and wait on the veranda for him?'

'Yes,' he whispered, even though the thought of leaving her side terrified him.

'When the doctor comes, bring him to me,' she said wearily. Then, with a soft moan, she turned and she swayed dizzily back to the bedroom, one hand pressed against her pale lips as if she feared she might throw up.

To Jake's horror, as he watched through the bedroom doorway, she collapsed onto the bed and lay perfectly, terribly still.

Petrified, he ignored her order to wait on the veranda. He raced into her bedroom and shook her gently, trying to wake her. Crying and sobbing, he shook her roughly, begging her, but still she wouldn't wake.

Then he saw the tiny bundle…

He tiptoed, heart in his mouth, around the bed and saw the tiny face of a baby, wrapped in a shawl, lying so close to the edge of the bed it could have fallen off.

Its eyes were closed and when he picked it up he touched its little face. It was cold and fear leapt inside him like a gas flame.

If only the doctor would come. Or his father and Roy.

His tears fell on the little bundle as he gently placed it in the safety of the crib in the corner of his parents' bedroom. And then he pulled a blanket over his mother and went to wait all alone on the veranda.

Only in the darkest of nightmares had Jake revisited the terror and misery of that long, lonely vigil. But now the shock of Mattie's pregnancy had torn down his careful defences and he couldn't hold back the black memories.

So many times during that night he'd crept back to the bedroom, praying that his mother or the baby would wake.

It was hours before the men had arrived, but at last they'd come. The flying doctor plane's lights had bobbed and bounced on the rough landing strip at around the same time the thunder of horses' hooves signalled the stockmen's return.

The doctor and Jake's father had gone straight to his mother, closing the door, and it was into Roy's arms that Jake had crumpled.

It was Roy who'd finally told him that his mother was going to be all right, but his baby brother had died. It was Roy who'd never left his side throughout the rest of that night or the next day. It was Roy who'd explained about premature stillbirth, Roy who'd assured Jake that he wasn't to blame for any of this. There was nothing he could have done.

A jagged groan broke from Jake and he slumped behind the steering wheel, staring through the windscreen at the pouring rain.

Now, as a rational adult, he knew his mother's experience wasn't common. She'd been a tragic victim of the Outback's isolation. Pregnancy in a huge city like Sydney was a totally different kettle of fish.

But an irrational corner of his heart shrank, chilled by the old fear he'd never quite been able to bury. He never wanted to put himself through that level of turmoil again.

Thankfully he'd had the sense to distance himself from Mattie, to walk out of her flat. If he'd stayed there he might have done something he'd regret, might have asked more questions, got himself more deeply entangled.

But how *could* a young woman get herself involved in something like this? How could she take such risks with her body for someone else?

You know why. Mattie Carey isn't just any girl.

Too true.

That was his problem.

Mattie was so much more than any girl he'd ever known... She wasn't just divinely sexy in silk and lace lingerie... She was warm, vibrant, special... She had a heart as big as...

Damn. If he went down that track, he'd start to feel involved and overly protective and he'd already decided that this was *not* his responsibility. He didn't want to be involved.

Slotting the key in the car's ignition, he started the engine, determined to put distance between himself and Mattie's pregnancy.

At the first junction, however, when he braked for a red light, his mind threw up pictures of Mattie over the next few months. Carrying twins.

The rapidly growing babies were going to be a huge drain on her. And who would be there to support her?

Did she know what could happen? Did she really think she could manage everything on her own? Why on earth was she doing this? Alone?

So many questions.

So many things to worry about.

Jake drove on, but the thought of Mattie going into labour and delivering twins sent his angry fist smashing into the steering wheel.

This surrogacy gesture was going too far. It was a one-way street with no chance to turn back. And now it was too late to talk her out of it. He felt as helpless now as he had when he was nine.

And he didn't want to get involved.

But did he have any other option?

Mattie needed help.

Without consciously making the decision, Jake circled the block until he was in front of the flats again. And then he was out of the car, dashing through the rain once more, this time without his coat.

He knocked an impatient tattoo on Mattie's front door, and the little dog barked madly. Again.

Again, Mattie took ages to open the door but, when she did, Jake felt as if he'd been slugged in the solar plexus.

Her eyes were red and watery and her nose was red too, as if she'd blown it many times. She was clutching a handful of damp tissues and, as soon as she saw him, she gave a hiccupping sob and her eyes filled with fresh tears.

'Mattie, I…'

She shook her head and pressed the wad of tissues against her mouth.

A strangling sensation seized Jake by the throat. He couldn't bear to think he'd done this to her. If anyone else had hurt Mattie Carey he would have cracked them on the jaw.

'I had to make sure you were OK,' he said. 'But I see you're not.'

Instead of inviting him in, she rolled her eyes and the action sent shiny tears spilling down her flushed cheeks. Hastily, she dashed them away with the heel of her hand. 'I've already told you I'm fine, Jake. You don't have to worry about me.'

She obviously didn't want to talk about her crying, so he tried another tack. 'Who's looking after you?'

'I don't need looking after.' Mattie blew her nose noisily

and wiped the last of her tears onto her sleeve. 'I'm not ill. Just pregnant.'

'But you're doing all this by yourself?'

'Pregnancy isn't exactly something you can share.'

She was being deliberately stubborn, which meant she was almost certainly angry. Battling his own impatience, Jake tried again. 'What about the next couple of months as the pregnancy advances?'

'When I'm as huge as two houses?'

'You're still going to have to shop and to cook, and to go to medical appointments.'

'Yes, but don't worry. I'll carry one of those warning signs: Oversize Load.'

He groaned in exasperation. 'Mattie, be serious. Don't tell me you're going to try to do this all on your own.'

'Why not? It's the truth.' She was beginning to sound bored by his interrogation.

Jake drew a deep breath and prayed for patience. 'You're expecting twins. Another *couple's* twins. Surely they owe you something? In my book they owe you big time, but it looks like they've abandoned you.'

'You don't know anything about them.' Mattie was calmer now. Calmer and colder. She stood, blocking the doorway, with her arms folded over her 'baby bump'. 'No one has abandoned me, Jake.'

As she said this her face fell, but she quickly recovered. 'It was my idea to come to Sydney. If I'd stayed in Willowbank, the whole town would have been trying to guess what was going on.'

She paused to blow her nose again and gave him a very deliberate, if watery, smile. 'I'm quite capable of managing alone and this is the way I want it. I couldn't handle the constant fussing if I'd stayed near Gina and Tom. They'd always be hovering over me, making sure I was OK.'

And so they should, Jake thought. *Anything might happen.*

He grimaced, fighting flashes of fear. 'But twins, Mattie. Surely you'll get too tired to look after this place and…and everything else?'

'All taken care of. Gina and Tom have sent me a lovely cleaner. She's brilliant. And they've even talked about a home delivery grocery service.'

This was good news at least. 'So they are looking after you?'

'They've showered me with all kinds of pampering.' She held out her hands, displaying her glamorous nails. 'They've sent me vouchers for manicures, facials, massages, pedicures. They're spoiling me rotten.'

'Right.'

Mattie folded her arms again and stood with her head resolutely high and her shoulders back, as if she'd donned armour and could now face any foe. 'Thanks for checking, Jake. It was sweet of you to worry.'

He gulped. 'No problem.'

She reached for the door, as if their conversation had come to a close and she wanted him to leave.

He felt suddenly deprived of oxygen.

'Wait,' he said sharply. He wanted to tell her that she mustn't cry and that he…that he…

What?

Panic gripped him. What was his role here?

Mattie didn't need his practical support. He was anxious to avoid emotional attachment. Seduction wasn't on the agenda. All the ground rules had changed for him. He didn't have a role.

Mattie was watching him expectantly, one hand on the door, ready to pull it shut.

He gulped, didn't know what to do next. It was unbelievable. Jake Devlin, on a woman's doorstep, lost for words. In desperation, he said, 'You've left out the cat.'

'I beg your pardon?' She frowned. 'What are you talking about? I don't have a cat. Only Brutus.'

'No. In the drawing of Molly, the little witch. You usually have a black cat on every page.'

Mattie turned slowly and a small frown made vertical tracks in her forehead as she looked across the lounge room to the table with her art gear. Jake held his breath as he studied her profile.

He could see the dusty fringe of her lashes, the tiny bump on her nose, the warm curves of her lips, soft as petals. The hairdresser's highlights had faded from her hair, leaving it a gentle light brown. Not mousy at all, but exactly the right colour for her.

He was remembering how her lips had tasted, how eagerly they'd parted for him. To his surprise, her ripening body hadn't diminished his desire. He longed to hold her, to touch her.

'You're absolutely right,' she said. 'I've forgotten to put the little cat in the last drawing. I suppose I can blame maternity amnesia.'

She turned to him again, her expression puzzled and wary.

Jake struggled to remember what they'd been talking about. Not her lips. Oh, yeah, the cat. 'He could…uh…he could be hiding under the table.'

Mattie smiled. 'Yes, I could show him half-hidden by a corner of the tablecloth and waiting for Molly to pass him a piece of mackerel.'

Jake nodded. 'Something like that.'

Her eyes glowed with sudden warmth, the heart-stopping warmth he remembered, and he wondered how she would react if he tried to kiss her now.

Should he kiss her now?

'That's a really good idea, Jake. Thank you for reminding me about that cat. My little readers would have been mortified if I'd left him out.'

'You're welcome.'

She dropped her gaze to her rounded stomach, gave a sigh, then lifted her gaze again. 'Is that all, Jake?'

No!

The urge to kiss her was all consuming. But, in the past, Jake's kisses had almost always led to seduction and now he yearned for something else. Something more, something deeper, better.

He needed Mattie in ways he'd never needed anyone before. Whenever he was with her he felt happy and strangely content. When he was away from her he was dismal and worried for no reason. But he had no idea how to tell her that. More importantly, he didn't want to admit it to himself.

The very thought that his happiness depended on a pregnant woman was beyond terrifying.

Mattie began to pull the door shut and, through the narrowing space, she looked out at him, her blue eyes huge and wistful. 'Give my love to Roy.'

'Sure,' Jake said, but he knew that he couldn't just walk away. Mattie needed him. He had no idea how to care for her but, God help him, he had to try.

Years ago, his mother had exiled him to the veranda. Now Mattie was pregnant and he couldn't contemplate a similar self-imposed exile.

He took an anxious step forward, but Mattie said calmly,
'All the best, Jake. I hope you enjoy your leave.'

And she closed the door.

CHAPTER EIGHT

AT LEAST, Mattie tried to close the door, but Jake was too fast for her.

With the speed of a tackling footballer, he blocked the narrowing gap.

She gave a startled cry. 'What are you trying to do? Lose an arm?'

He shrugged this question aside and shouldered the door wider open. 'I can't leave you like this. You're being far too stubborn.'

'*I'm* being stubborn?'

'You are if you think you can do this without help, Mattie.' His tone edged towards anger.

Mattie was angry too. 'You can't just barge in here and start bossing me around.'

Ignoring this, he strode past her into the flat.

Breathless with surprise, she followed him. 'I don't want you here, Jake.'

He came to a stop in the middle of the room and looked suddenly lost, like a small boy in trouble.

Mattie's soft heart began to melt.

'Look,' he said, running a hand over his face. 'I must

admit I'm thinking on my feet at the moment. I don't have a plan, but I can't…I can't…'

His beautiful face was pale and taut but, as he looked at Mattie, his mouth tilted into an uneven smile that did terrible things to the rhythm of her heart. 'I can't just walk out of here as if I don't give two hoots what happens to you, Mattie.'

For a moment she was too confused to speak. What exactly was he saying?

Her only truly coherent thought was that it would be rather nice if Jake wanted to take her in his arms and kiss her. But he wasn't offering kisses and she certainly wasn't going to ask him for one. She had tried that once before and the very thought of where that kiss had led to made her distinctly dizzy and light-headed.

'I need to sit down,' she said, sinking inelegantly onto a sofa.

'Of course.' Jake waited till she was comfortable, with a cushion at her back, before he sat on the sofa opposite.

Leaning forward, elbows on his knees, he clasped his hands and looked at her intently. 'I know next to nothing about women expecting twins.'

He looked so worried, she couldn't help smiling. 'Does any bachelor know about twin pregnancy unless he's studying obstetrics?'

Momentarily his face cleared and she caught a fleeting smile, but he quickly sobered. 'Listen, Mattie, I don't plan to make a nuisance of myself. I won't hang around here at the flat. I'll find somewhere else to stay and I'll give you plenty of space, but I'm going to be here in Sydney.'

'While you're on leave?'

'Until the twins are born.'

Mattie's jaw sagged.

'Why?' she finally managed to ask.

'I...I want to spend more time with Roy. And I can keep an eye on you at the same time.'

This didn't make sense. 'I don't need a watchdog, Jake. I have a perfectly good doctor.'

Jake was on his feet again, pacing the room like a caged lion. 'Look, I know you want me to keep my distance, so I don't want to crowd you.' He almost glared at her. 'But someone's got to keep an eye on you.'

Too surprised to speak, she sat looking up at him like a small bird hypnotised by a deadly handsome snake.

'I'll stay at the Dockside Apartments at Woolloomooloo,' he told her.

'But what about your job?' she remembered to ask.

'I'll get special leave. I'll resign if I have to.'

'But that's mad.'

He shook his head. 'I'll give you my mobile number and I want you to call me any time.'

'Call you?'

Frowning, he nodded. 'Any heavy lifting, call me. You want the dog walked, I'm your man. If you give me a list, I'll do your shopping for you. Anything breaks down— from the toaster to the air conditioner—let me sort it out. I'm probably better at dealing with tradesmen than you are.'

Mattie opened her mouth but no sound emerged. Why was he doing this? What did it mean? If Jake had been a proper boyfriend, she might have been charmed by his desire to help. But he was a man she'd slept with once, a man who couldn't commit. In fact, he was the man she was trying to forget!

At last she found her tongue. 'This is very kind, Jake, but I don't need to be wrapped in cotton wool.'

The muscles in his throat rippled. 'Just keep well, Mattie. Get plenty of rest and look after yourself. Let me know if there are any concerns.'

'But…I don't understand. Why are you doing this?'

His eyes flashed darkly. 'I don't like to see a pregnant woman trying to manage on her own.' A spasm jerked in his jaw and he clenched his teeth hard. Clenched his hands too.

Was there something deep-seated behind this unexpected urge to protect her? A secret in Jake's past? A pregnant woman in trouble? Mattie longed to ask, but Jake seemed so different now, so stern and masterful, and she was just a little afraid of him.

He exhaled slowly. 'So,' he said, 'I'd better give you my contact details.'

'Oh, yes…right.' Mattie had to wriggle her bottom towards the edge of the sofa before she could stand.

Jake was suddenly beside her, offering a strong hand at her elbow, supporting her as she stood. His touch sent a wave of heat flashing through her.

'Thank you.' Her voice was breathless and faint. 'I'll just get my little black book from the kitchen.'

'Hey, stranger.' Will's voice sounded jovial on the other end of the line. 'I didn't expect to hear from you. How's your leave?'

Flopped on a sofa in his Woolloomooloo apartment, Jake stared at the ceiling as he answered. 'It hasn't gone quite to plan.'

'Don't tell me the world's run out of beautiful, available women?'

'Something like that.' Truth be told, Jake hadn't even tried to pick up another woman—an unheard-of phenomenon. 'I'm staying on here,' he said. 'That's why I've rung. I've told the boss I'm not coming back and I need you to pack up my things, if you don't mind.'

'You're joking. What's happened? Are you OK?'

'Yeah, sure. I just need to stay here. At least for the next couple of months. Maybe then, if there's a position available...' He let the words trail off.

Seconds of silence ticked by. Will said, 'Does this have anything to do with Mattie Carey?'

'Mattie? What makes you ask that?'

'I had a weird e-mail from her.'

Zap! Jake cleared his throat. 'What did she say?'

'It seems she's worried about you.'

'That's a joke, right?'

'Not at all. She sounded seriously concerned. She didn't tell me you'd resigned, though.'

'I'm fine,' Jake said but, even to his ears, he didn't sound convincing.

'So, what's going on between you and Mattie?'

'Very little.'

'Pull the other one.'

Jake let out a heavy sigh. He'd had enough trouble yesterday, steering Roy away from discussions about Mattie.

'I must say I was surprised.' Will sounded as if he was settling in for a lengthy chat. 'I wouldn't have thought Mattie Carey was your type.'

Jake resisted the urge to rise to his friend's bait. His resistance lasted maybe all of five seconds. Then he had to ask. 'So, why isn't Mattie my type?'

Will laughed. 'You know very well how you like your women.'

'You tell me.'

'Ready, willing and able.'

Normally, a comment like this wouldn't have fazed Jake. Today it sent a blast of embarrassing heat scorching the back of his neck. *Damn.* He'd stumbled straight into this trap.

From down the phone line, he could hear the dawning suspicion in his mate's voice. 'Jake, you didn't.'

Jake tried to ignore him.

Will persisted. 'Tell me it's not true. That week when you shared the flat with Mattie, you didn't—'

'Give it a miss, Will.'

'But—' Will whistled softly. 'Not you and Mattie?'

'It's none of your business.' Jake clenched a threatening fist and unclenched it again. Took a calming breath. 'Anyway, it's rather late for you to be talking to me about Mattie Carey.' He spoke in his driest tone. 'You're supposed to be my best mate and you knew she was planning to get herself pregnant with someone else's kids, but you kindly overlooked sharing that minor detail with me.'

'It was a delicate matter, Jake. A private arrangement between Mattie and my sister and her husband. As far as you were concerned, I was working on a need to know basis. How did I know that you needed to know?'

'I asked you enough questions.'

'Yeah, but I thought that was nothing more than idle curiosity. I never occurred to me—I didn't dream you and Mattie were an item.'

'We're not.'

'Then why's she so bothered about you?'

'Because…because she's Mattie. She's bothered about every living thing on this planet.'

'That's very true.'

'Saint Matilda,' Jake growled.

'Or not so saintly, it would seem?'

'Shut up.'

'OK, OK.'

'I'd really appreciate it if you could pack up my things.'

'Sure. No problem.'

Tom thumped Mattie's kitchen table with his fist. 'Jack wins hands down as the boy's name.'

Gina shook her head. 'Jack's too traditional. Don't we want something trendier, like Jasper or Jake?' She turned to Mattie, who'd almost spilled her cup of peppermint tea at the mention of Jake. 'Don't you agree?'

Mattie shook her head. 'I d-don't think you should include me in a discussion of names.'

To her surprise, Gina and Tom responded in unison. 'Why not?'

She forced a smile. 'They're your babies. The two of you will have enough trouble reaching agreement. If I stick my oar in, you'll never be able to decide.'

Gina was clearly disappointed. 'I can't imagine not including you, Mattie. Gosh, you and I have been talking about babies' names since we were in primary school.'

Mattie patted her protruding tummy. 'But we're dealing with real babies now. Yours and Tom's. And they'll be stuck with the names you choose for the rest of their lives.'

'Of course, I know that.'

Trying to lighten the atmosphere, Mattie said, 'I've been calling them Dot and Dash.' But Gina, who'd obviously lost her sense of humour, continued to look unhappy.

Relenting, Mattie squeezed her friend's hand. 'All right, if you must know, I hope you don't call your little boy Jake.'

'Why? Don't you like Jake?'

Mattie smothered an urge to sigh. Of course she liked the name Jake. She was very fond of Jake. Too fond and way too sentimental. Just hearing the name brought her to the brink of tears.

Jake Devlin was confusing her to distraction. He'd been kind, yes, but she still didn't really understand what was behind his urge to protect her. There were times when she thought that he truly cared about her, but he remained so careful and distant she couldn't be sure.

Deep down, where the scars left by Pete had never properly healed, Mattie had to admit she was scared. And she was probably confusing Jake as much as he confused her. She'd held him at bay so many times he assumed that was what she wanted. Who could blame him?

If neither of them was ready to open up, she might never get to the bottom of what was going on between them. But if Gina and Tom called their little boy Jake, she'd be hearing his name for the rest of her life, an eternal reminder of this painful, puzzling interlude.

Gina, meanwhile, was waiting for her answer.

'Look…this is why I shouldn't be involved,' Mattie said. 'Don't take any notice of me. Jake's a fine name.'

Gina watched her thoughtfully for several seconds and then her expression cleared.

'*Oh,*' she said with dramatic emphasis. 'I should have remembered. That hot guy who stayed with you here last summer—Will's friend—his name was Jake, wasn't it?'

Mattie winced.

'He broke your heart,' Gina announced dramatically.

'My heart's perfectly sound.'

'But you really fancied him.'

Mattie answered with a shrug.

Gina sighed. 'You poor thing. I'm sure Will told me once that Jake went through women like water.' She rolled her eyes. 'Some men have a lot to answer for.'

This discussion was rather more than Mattie could bear. She didn't want to tell Gina and Tom that Jake was back in Sydney, planning to hover in the distance and watch over her like some kind of anxious guardian angel.

They would want details. Answers. She didn't have answers.

With a deliberately casual shrug, she defended Jake. 'Look, it wasn't all one-sided. It was as much my fault as his.'

'Which means we should drop the subject,' said Tom firmly as he gave his wife a warning glance.

'Hmm,' said Gina.

'We don't want to say anything to upset Mattie,' Tom insisted. 'We shouldn't be raising her stress levels over naming the babies. That's why she's come to Sydney—to be spared all that.'

Tom looked so concerned and fatherly that Mattie thought, for a moment, he was going to lean over and place a hand on her forehead to test her temperature.

But, to her relief, he refrained. And Gina took the hint and gave up the discussion of baby names.

Mattie sat at the card table by the window, typing on her laptop. She was supposed to be working on the final version of Molly's story, but she found it hard to concentrate. Jake had called to ask if she was free because he wanted to visit her and, ever since his call, she'd been in a tailspin.

Carol, her neighbour, breezed past on her way back from the letter box and she doubled back to stop at Mattie's window.

She let out a low wolf whistle. 'You're looking swish today. Expecting a special visitor?'

'Not really.' Mattie tried to sound airy about the fact that she was wearing her prettiest maternity top and two layers of mascara, but she promptly spoiled it by blushing.

Carol smiled knowingly, then glanced out to the street where a car was pulling up. 'This not-really-special visitor wouldn't be male and about six feet three, would he?'

Mattie blushed again. 'Possibly.'

Grinning broadly now, Carol began to fan herself with her mail. 'Call the hospital Emergency,' she panted theatrically. 'I'm having palpitations.'

Mattie laughed, but then she heard footsteps on the front path and, sure enough, it was Jake who was heading her way and her heart began to quicken too.

Carol disappeared and suddenly Jake was knocking on her front door.

'Behave, Brutus,' Mattie ordered and, to her relief, the little dog obeyed her.

She opened the door and saw that Jake had made an effort with his appearance too. He was impeccably dressed in an open-necked blue chambray shirt and dark trousers, and his sleek tan boots were very well polished. She felt a rush of longing. Good heavens. She hadn't thought it was possible to be heavily pregnant with twins and still feel this kind of wanting.

He kept his hands behind his back, as if he was hiding something.

'Good morning, Mattie.' His deep voice rippled over her like sexy music, and he smiled shyly as he brought his hands in front of him to reveal two potted plants—a small rose bush, covered with the sweetest miniature pink blooms, and a cluster of irises, with frilled petals as deep blue as a mid-summer sky.

'They're in honour of your babies,' he said with a shy smile.

'They're gorgeous,' Mattie whispered. 'Pink for the girl, blue for the boy.' Her eyes swam with tears. *Stop it. Stop it right now.*

'I thought you might prefer living plants to cut flowers.'

She nodded her thanks, and sniffed. She was over-whelmed. 'I…I'll put the kettle on.'

'No, you won't. You'll stay here and I'll put the kettle on.'

'Jake!' She rolled her eyes at him. 'Honestly, I'm fit as a—'

'Yeah, I know,' he interrupted, smiling. 'You're as fit as three fiddles, but humour me, Mattie. I've been to the library and I've read up on expecting twins. You're supposed to take it easy in the last trimester. So now it's my turn to be the helpful type and you'll have to accept it graciously. Put your feet up and stay on that sofa.'

To cover her surprise, she said meekly, 'All right. I'll have peppermint tea, please. The tea bags are in the blue pot with the wooden lid.'

Taking him at his word, she kicked her sandals off and made herself comfortable on the sofa with her feet up.

But she couldn't relax.

Jake's behaviour was too bewildering.

It was so hard to reconcile the man in her kitchen fixing her herbal tea with the man she'd first met. She kept seeing Ange's knickers on the bathroom floor and those tangled bed sheets.

And then, no sooner had Ange been out of the picture, than Jake had leapt into Mattie's bed.

She couldn't stop thinking about that awful farewell at the airport: *You do know that I can't promise you a future together, don't you?*

When he'd returned to Mongolia, she'd realised that everything about Jake Devlin had pointed to one dangerous fact—he was a playboy.

Now he was trying to protect her.

It was all terribly confusing.

Anyone looking from the outside might reasonably assume that a man who'd given up his job to hang about, waiting to help and support a pregnant woman, must care deeply about her. Mattie would have liked to believe that too, but it was so hard to believe that a man who obviously loved to play the field would still find her attractive when she was the size of a whale.

Her entire life these days was dominated by the babies. She was sure she could feel her hips actually spreading. She needed to go the bathroom every five minutes and her ankles swelled if she was on her feet for too long.

She now had weekly visits to the doctor and the babies' progress was being strictly monitored, which meant there were times when she truly felt exactly the way Jake had described her—like an incubator.

She'd begun to wonder if she could ever change back into the reckless, happy girl who'd shared this flat with Jake.

That special day when they'd brewed billy tea for Roy and had gone to the movies seemed so very long ago. As for their one passionate night—that perfect, blissful night—it now felt as if it had happened in another lifetime.

Mattie hoped she didn't look too anxious when Jake returned with her tea and a mug of instant coffee for himself.

To her surprise, he didn't sit opposite her.

Looking super-relaxed and totally in charge, he sat on the end of her sofa, mere inches from her bare feet.

The sofa cushion dipped with his weight. His knee brushed her leg and heat rushed over her in a sweeping flash. It wasn't fair! He looked so cool, while she was taking so many deep breaths she was in danger of hyperventilating.

'Have you seen Roy lately?' she asked breathlessly.

Jake nodded. 'I'm a bit worried about him, actually. I don't think he's very well.'

'Really? I'm sorry to hear that. Have you spoken to the staff at the nursing home?'

'They assure me he's as well as can be expected, but to me he looks like he has one foot in the grave.'

'Poor darling.'

Jake's dark eyes rested on Mattie. For the longest time he watched her. 'You look well,' he said softly. 'Actually, you look—'

'Blooming?'

He laughed. 'I was thinking of something more flattering.' *Really?*

Mattie held her breath, but Jake had apparently decided to change the subject. 'So what happens to Brutus and Pavarotti when you go into hospital? Who's going to look after them?'

'Gina and Tom will collect them some time next week, in case anything happens early.'

'Early?'

'It can happen with twins.'

'Yes, so I've discovered.'

'At the library?'

Jake nodded. He was frowning deeply and his eyes had turned stony as he glared at a spot on the carpet.

'Anyway,' Mattie continued, hoping to distract him, 'Gina and Tom will take Brutus and Pavarotti back to Willowbank, and I think Gina's parents will probably look after them.'

He nodded and then reached into his trouser pocket. 'I bought something for your menagerie.' With a smile, he produced a blue rubber fetch-and-play toy in the shape of a bone. He held it out to Brutus. 'This is for you, chum.'

The little dog immediately went into paroxysms of delight, rolling and wrestling with the rubber bone.

'Jake, it's perfect. He loves it.'

Jake dug into his other pocket and pulled out something that looked like a twig with a pretty hanging mobile attached.

Mattie laughed. 'Is that for Pavarotti?'

'Yes. It's a pedicure perch.'

'A what?'

'A pedicure perch.' His dark eyes sparkled. 'Pavarotti can wrap his little claws around this stick and peck at the mobile and have a pedicure at the same time.'

She laughed so hard she almost hiccuped. 'Wow!' she said between giggles. 'That's outrageous, but I love it.'

Without warning, Mattie stopped in mid-giggle. For a minute there, she'd let go of her doubts and fears. She'd been as happy as she had been in those first few days with Jake. They'd packed so much into their short time together. The laughter, the happiness—the passion.

Jake had warned her that it couldn't last.

That was still true. It couldn't last, could it?

She had to ask. 'Jake, why are you doing this?'

'Doing what?'

She held up the perch. 'Why are you here? Why are you

being so thoughtful?' She gulped. Oh, heavens. She mustn't get teary in front of him.

For a long moment he seemed caught out, as if he didn't know how to answer her. Mattie could see his mind working and it was almost as if he was asking himself the same question.

He stared at her, his face serious, almost worried. He dropped his gaze to Brutus, pouncing on his blue rubber bone. 'Remember the day we took Roy out and we brewed billy tea?'

'Yes, of course.'

'I realised then that you're always going the extra mile to make other people happy, but I wondered if anyone ever does that for you.'

The little perch trembled in Mattie's hand. 'Is that what this is about? You're trying to make me happy?'

Jake smiled. 'That's the aim.'

'Oh!'

Mattie couldn't help it.

She burst into tears.

In a heartbeat, Jake's arms were around her and she was sobbing against his big solid shoulder. But he didn't seem to mind. He kissed her forehead and stroked her hair and made soothing noises the way a parent might.

She clung to him—she had no choice—she was collapsing beneath the weight of her emotions. She was happy, sad, confused, scared, but, somewhere within the disarray, she knew that she loved this man.

Even though it was dangerous, and he might break her heart, she loved everything about him. Right now, she could smell his skin and his aftershave and his laundered shirt and the combination was wonderful.

'Mattie,' he murmured hoarsely, 'you mustn't cry. I didn't want to upset you.'

There was a sudden knock at the open front door. 'What's going on?'

It was Tom's voice.

CHAPTER NINE

TOM was like a soldier on sentry duty as he stood stiffly in the doorway, red hair standing up in spikes, frowning at them. 'What's happened? Are you all right, Mattie?'

Her face was flooded with tears, her throat was too tight for speech and her shoulders were shaking from the force of her sobbing. All she could manage was to nod her head vigorously.

Tom marched into the flat, jaw at a belligerent angle. 'Are you sure you're OK? What's going on here?' He shot a scalding glare at Jake. 'Excuse me, but who are you?'

Slowly Jake rose from the sofa and the air in the small lounge room was suddenly thick with tension and testosterone. Jake was a head taller than Tom and he looked ready for a battle.

Without smiling, he held out his hand. 'Jake Devlin's the name. How do you do?'

'Jake, this is Tom,' Mattie supplied in a choked voice. 'Tom Roberts.'

The two men shook hands grimly.

Jake said quietly and without warmth, 'So, you're the babies' father?'

'That's right.' Tom squared his shoulders. 'And I've

heard about you—Our Man in Mongolia.' He spoke the way a policeman might address a hardened criminal.

Jake slid a smooth, questioning glance Mattie's way.

'Jake's a friend, Tom,' she intervened. 'A…a good friend.'

'But he has a habit of upsetting you?'

'Not at all,' she insisted. 'Jake hasn't upset me.' She pointed to the plants on the coffee table. 'He's brought me lovely gifts.'

Tom eyed the plants suspiciously and Mattie surreptitiously wiped at her tears with the corner of a handkerchief. She noticed black smudges of mascara on the white fabric and she hoped she hadn't ended up with panda eyes.

'I didn't know you were back in Sydney, Tom.' She was pleased she could speak more calmly now. 'Is Gina here too?'

He shook his head. 'I had to come to town for a quick business trip and I couldn't come without popping in to see you.' He looked again at the potted plants and shot Jake a sharp-eyed glance.

'Why don't you take a seat?' Jake suggested dryly and he sat again on the sofa beside Mattie, so close that his shirt sleeve brushed her arm, and her skin flashed hot and cold.

She hoped Tom would stop bristling and be pleasant to Jake, but she was out of luck.

As soon as Tom was seated, he attacked Jake. 'I presume Mattie's told you she's expecting twins?'

'Of course.'

'And has she also told you that many women expecting twins have to spend their last trimester in hospital to ensure they have sufficient rest?'

Mattie didn't dare to look at Jake, but she could feel his tension.

Tom pressed his point home. 'In other words, Mattie mustn't be upset.'

'Tom, I can reassure you,' Jake said smoothly. 'I want nothing more than for Mattie to be rested and well and to have a safe delivery.'

Tom gave a slight nod of acknowledgement, but his expression was still doubtful.

Diplomatically, Mattie asked, 'How's Gina?'

'Fabulous.' At last Tom smiled. 'Apart from the fact that she talks about the babies all day long and half the night and then in her sleep as well.'

Mattie smiled. 'She's a tad excited, isn't she?'

'Excited? There ought to be a better word.'

Jake rose. 'I should go,' he said. 'I'm sure you two want to have a good long chat.'

'There's no need to leave,' Mattie began, but Jake looked determined so she didn't push it.

He turned to Tom, gave a stiffly polite nod. 'Nice to meet you.'

'You too,' Tom replied without conviction.

'See you later, Mattie.' Jake bent down and kissed her cheek. His mouth only brushed her skin briefly, but her heart leapt as high as the moon and she was sure his lips left a scorch mark.

She wanted to tell him that he was welcome to drop by any time, but with Tom frowning ferociously, as if he were guarding her like one of his sheepdogs, she held her tongue.

'Thanks for the gifts, Jake. They're gorgeous.'

'My pleasure. Take care.'

When Jake left she felt as if all the fun had gone out of her day. It took a huge effort to paste on a smile for Tom's benefit.

'I hope he's not going to make a habit of upsetting you,' Tom said even before Jake's footsteps had died away.

'He won't,' Mattie assured him, but she couldn't be sure it was the truth. She was simply a mess where he was concerned.

For the babies' sake, she should snap out of it.

What a stuff-up.

Jake couldn't believe he'd made such a hash of visiting Mattie. As he stormed to his car he felt so fired up and mad with himself he wanted to kick something.

He'd gone in there all gung-ho and he'd ended up with Mattie in tears. As if that wasn't bad enough, when the babies' father had arrived, he'd very nearly started an argument with him.

Our Man in Mongolia. That was below the belt.

Then again…

Jake slowed his pace as he tried to sort out what had just happened.

Truth be told, Tom probably had good reason to be so upset. He must have had a shock when he'd turned up at the flat expecting to see the woman who was carrying his children resting up safely and serenely, only to find her in another bloke's arms, sobbing her heart out.

Give the man a break.

Yeah, maybe.

Even so, Jake couldn't shrug the incident aside. He'd been on the brink of some kind of breakthrough.

OK, so Mattie had been weeping in his arms, but if they'd been given half a chance, her tears might have broken down barriers and he might have begun to make some kind of sense of the turmoil inside him.

Then good old Tom had barged in like the SAS saving the world.

Jake pressed his car's central locking device and, as he heard the lock's *click-click,* he remembered Mattie's question.

Why are you doing this?

He'd told her that he wanted to help her, but that was only half the truth, wasn't it? And even then he'd made her cry.

Just as well he hadn't told her the rest—that he was starting to realise that he needed to be with her, that she was the best thing that had ever happened to him.

If he'd told her that, she might have expected a promise of some kind of serious commitment—a confession that he loved her, that he was ready for marriage and a family of their own. But how could he be?

That was going too far. Way too far.

It was downright terrifying.

The true answer was that Jake was taking this venture one step at a time. One day at a time. He didn't dare to look any further ahead and how could he tell Mattie that?

Perhaps, after all, he should be grateful to Tom for barging in when he had.

Jake was asleep when the phone rang. His first thought as he swung out of bed was Mattie. Panic kicked him in the chest. Had something happened to her? He groped in the dark for his phone.

'Mr Devlin?'

'Speaking.'

'It's Sister Hart from the Lilydale Nursing Home.'

'Yes? What is it? Is Roy OK?'

'I'm afraid I have bad news. Roy's had a heart attack.'

Whack! Jake felt as if his own heart had been chopped

with an axe. 'How—' His throat was dry and he had to swallow. 'How is he?'

'It's quite serious. He's been taken to hospital, of course, so you'll need to ring the Coronary Care Unit to check on his condition.'

'Right.' Already Jake's mind was racing. He wouldn't simply telephone. He'd drive straight to the hospital. He knew the first few hours after a heart attack were crucial. He had to try to see Roy.

It was the early hours of the morning, still dark, as he drove through the Sydney streets. His hands were sweaty on the steering wheel and fear gnawed at his stomach and clutched at his throat. He loved Roy and he couldn't bear it if he died.

He accepted that Roy couldn't live for ever, but he felt a nagging sense of injustice on Roy's behalf. The guy was a legend. He deserved a hero's old age.

Jake drove through the hospital's multilevel car park, eyes alert for an empty parking spot. His fear spiralled as he hurried through the maze of disinfected corridors to the Coronary Care Unit. He'd steeled himself for the grimness of the ward, the hushed atmosphere, the frightening banks of blinking lights and the frowning scrutiny of the nursing sister in charge, but he couldn't stop blaming himself.

I should have done more. Please, don't let it be too late.

Mid-afternoon, Mattie's heart leapt when her phone rang and she saw Jake's name on her caller ID.

'I'm sorry,' he said. 'I've only just found all your messages. I had the phone switched off.'

'I forgive you.' She tried to sound light-hearted and failed dismally. The fact that Jake hadn't answered her messages had frightened her.

It brought back memories of dating Pete. So many times she'd tried to ring him in Perth and he hadn't been available. She'd probably developed some kind of complex about men and mobile phones.

'I've been at the hospital all day,' Jake said. 'Roy's had a heart attack.'

'Oh, no.' Mattie was instantly ashamed of herself. 'How is he?'

'They tell me he's holding his own.'

'I guess that's good news, then.'

'I guess. I'll feel better when I can speak to him.'

'Don't worry,' Mattie said gently. 'Roy's tough.'

'Yeah.' Jake sighed. 'Anyway, how are you?'

'Actually—' Mattie bit her lip. She wished now that she didn't have to tell Jake her news. 'I'm in hospital too.'

'What?' That single word echoed like a rifle shot.

'It's OK, Jake. It's not a code-orange alert. The doctor's simply taking precautions.'

'But why? What's wrong?'

'I started having contractions and he was worried I was going into early labour. The contractions have settled down, but I've been ordered complete bed rest.' She wrinkled her nose as she spoke into the phone. 'It means I have to stay in hospital until the babies are born.'

'Right.'

Jake sounded winded and Mattie felt sorry for him. Two medical dramas in one day was a coincidence no one welcomed. 'We want to give the babies the best possible chance,' she explained gently. 'Twins often come early.'

'Which hospital are you in?'

'Southmead.'

'The same hospital as Roy.' He made a sound that was almost a chuckle. 'At least that makes it easier for me to visit you both. Which ward?'

'I'll give you three guesses,' she said, smiling.

'Oh, yes, of course—Maternity. What room?'

'2203. But, Jake, I don't expect you to visit me when you're so worried about Roy.'

On the other end of the line, she heard Jake's sigh.

'You don't have a choice, Mattie.' His voice was deep, dark and insistent. 'I'm already on my way.'

Mattie's room was empty.

Jake stared at the vacant bed, at the rumpled sheets and the dent in the pillow where her head had lain. He saw the novel she'd been reading and an empty tea cup on the bedside table. He knew this was her room because, apart from its number, the pink rose bush and the blue irises sat on a small table under the window.

Everything looked normal but he felt uneasy. He'd been talking to her ten minutes ago. What could have happened in such a short time?

Crossing the room, he knocked on the door to the *en suite* bathroom, but there was no answer so he opened the door carefully. She wasn't there.

His heart began to thud. Hard. He rushed out of the room and down the corridor to the nurses' station.

A young woman greeted him with a beaming smile. 'How can I help you, sir?'

'Mattie Carey,' he gasped. 'She isn't in her room.'

The nurse's eyes twinkled and her face broke into a silly grin. Jake wanted to yell at her that this was serious.

'You must be Jake,' she said.

'Yes. Did Mattie leave a message?'

She nodded. 'She asked me to let you know they've taken her down to X-Ray.'

'Why? What's wrong?'

'Her doctor ordered another scan.'

A soft groan came from the back of Jake's throat and the nurse took pity on him. Her eyes softened. 'Don't worry, it's a routine procedure. Mattie shouldn't be too long.'

'Right.' He closed his eyes briefly and allowed himself to breathe. 'Thanks.' He took another breath. 'What do you suggest? Should I come back in…in about an hour, then?'

She nodded, then sighed. 'That's so sweet.'

'I beg your pardon?'

But the nurse had turned bright red and wouldn't answer him. She simply buried her nose in a bundle of charts.

Mattie lay on her side with her eyes closed, tired after the scan. Not that it had been a big deal, but everything seemed to make her tired these days. The nurse had told her that Jake had come while she was away. Poor guy.

What a rotten day he'd had.

She tried to shift into a more comfortable position.

She was such a sloth these days. An uncomfortable sloth. She was tired of being uncomfortable, tired of the babies kicking and head-butting her insides.

And now, after just one day, she was tired of the doctors and medical staff fussing over her, tired of the thought of spending day after day in this little white room.

Heavens, she'd become such a grouch. It was almost as if she and Jake had traded places. When they'd met, he'd been the grouchy one and now he was being sweet. So kind to Roy. To her.

But the other day, when she'd tried to talk to him about it, she'd asked him one question and then she'd burst into tears. Poor man.

It was strange that she'd leapt into bed with Jake without a second thought but, when it came to talking about their relationship, she was a mass of nerves. Perhaps that was Pete's legacy. He'd always hated talking about their future.

She was drifting off to sleep when she heard the soft tap-tap on her door, and she kept her eyes closed. She'd missed Jake's visit, but with any luck she might fall asleep and dream of him kissing her. It was so long ago that he'd kissed her. She wanted to remember exactly how his lips had felt on hers, how he'd tasted.

Perhaps, if she pretended to be asleep, the person at the door would give up and go away. So many people had interrupted her today to take her blood pressure, to give her steroid injections to strengthen the babies' lungs, to give her vitamin tablets, to bring her lunch, afternoon tea. Soon it would be time for supper.

She wasn't hungry.

'Mattie.'

Jake's voice.

Her eyes shot open.

He was in the doorway, looking at her with a worried, tender smile.

She struggled to sit up.

'I'm sorry if I woke you,' he said, coming into the room.

'I wasn't really asleep.' Her hair was falling all over her face and she tucked it behind her ear. 'I'm pleased to see you. Have a seat.'

Jake brought a chair close to the bed. It wasn't quite as nice as having him right beside her on a sofa, but Mattie wasn't about to complain.

'I came earlier,' he told her. 'But you were away having a scan. Is everything OK?'

'Yes, the babies are doing really well.'

'But you look tired.'

'It comes with the territory.'

He was watching her carefully.

'You've had a rotten day,' she said. 'I'm so sorry about Roy.'

'I think he's going to pull through. They're talking about an operation. Something called angioplasty—to open blocked coronary arteries.'

'How does Roy feel about that?'

'Resigned. He's not ready to shuffle off this mortal coil just yet.'

'I'm glad.'

Jake stared into her eyes for an immeasurable period of time. 'I suppose I should be pleased that you're here, where experts can keep an eye on you.'

'Yes, let them worry about me, Jake. You don't have to.'

'I can't help it.'

'Women have babies every day.'

'Of course they do.' He smiled, but she saw fear flicker deep in his eyes, quick as a fish's tail, then he looked away and pointed to the pot plants. 'You've brought them with you.'

'I had to. They're my good luck charms, although I can only water them with my tooth glass.'

'They're looking healthy so far.' Reaching over, he took her hands in his. 'You must have green thumbs.'

His thumbs stroked hers slowly and he smiled again and Mattie smiled back at him and she could feel her tiredness evaporating. For ages they didn't speak—simply held hands, smiling.

It was so long since they'd touched like this and it might have been awkward, but Mattie only felt a wonderful warmth, a sense of peace and of rightness, as if being with Jake was like coming home.

But he broke the magic by becoming practical again. 'Were you able to make plans for Brutus and Pavarotti?'

'Not yet, it was all so sudden. But thanks for reminding me. That was one of the reasons I was trying to ring you.'

He jumped in quickly. 'I'd be happy to drop over there and keep an eye on them. I can take Brutus for walks.'

'You should move into the flat,' Mattie said, wondering why she hadn't thought of it straight away. 'It's just sitting there empty.' Already, she was digging the keys out of a drawer in the bedside table. 'I know Will won't mind, and it's handy for the hospital. Easier for visiting Roy.'

'And you.'

She smiled. 'Exactly.'

As she handed Jake the keys he asked, 'So, how's the food here?'

'I…I haven't had much yet. I haven't been very hungry.'

'You should be eating for three, shouldn't you?'

'So I've been told.'

Watching her, Jake's thoughtful frown morphed into a slow smile. 'Why don't you have dinner with me tomorrow night?'

Her jaw dropped. 'I beg your pardon? How can I do that when I'm confined to barracks?'

'I know a terrific restaurant that does great gourmet

takeaways. I'll collect it and bring it here. We can have dinner together right here in this room.'

'Oh.'

For a horrifying moment, Mattie thought she might start to cry again. *I mustn't. I mustn't.*

Jake was waiting for her answer. 'What do you say? Do we have a date?'

It was a crime that he had to ask. As if a solitary meal of bland hospital food could possibly compete with any dinner with Jake. 'Thanks,' she whispered. 'I'd *love* to have dinner with you.'

'Terrific.' He stood, then reached down and gently touched her cheek. 'Now rest up, won't you? I'll see you tomorrow.'

As if she could rest now. She was way too excited.

Jake walked Brutus along the edge of the bay and dragged in deep breaths of fresh, salty air as he tried to relax. Not an easy task, given that he was up to his eyeballs in life and death dramas.

This morning Roy had been at death's door, now Mattie was about to give birth to not one, but *two* babies, and Jake was deeply involved in both incidents. Heavy going for a guy who'd been accused more than once of living in an emotional vacuum.

To cap it off, he'd asked Mattie to have dinner with him, which meant he was dating a woman who was pregnant with babies that weren't his—or hers. It was hard to get his head around.

In front of him now, the sun was melting into a golden puddle in the distant water. Seagulls screeched and squabbled. Small waves lapped at rocks. Jake drew another deep breath.

He should lighten up.

Things weren't so very bad, really. The doctors had told him that Roy would pull through, even though his face was still so ghostly pale it almost blended into the pillows. His old mate was being kept alive right now by IV drips and wires, as well as small TV screens with alarming green lines, but he was in good hands.

And, for that matter, Mattie was fine too…

He just had to keep taking one step at a time. He really had no other choice.

The dinner date was perfect—a superbly piquant coq au vin, followed by melt-in-the-mouth chocolate truffle cake, and sparkling mineral water in champagne flutes.

Mattie couldn't remember a meal she'd enjoyed more, but the evening went from fabulous to perfect when Jake kissed her.

It was so unexpected. One minute he was sitting beside her on the bed, laughing as they shared a joke, the next he was leaning in to her and his lips were teasing-soft as they brushed her cheek. He whispered her name and his mouth was warm on her skin, trailing kisses so light she could barely feel them.

'I'm allowed to kiss you, aren't I?' he whispered. 'I promise to be gentle.'

At first she was too stunned and breathless to answer.

'Mattie?'

She was shaking, but she managed to smile. 'I…I'm sure a gentle kiss is just what the doctor ordered.'

Indeed, her greedy skin was already shivering and yearning for more. Jake trailed kisses to her mouth and she closed her eyes. With gentle hands he cradled her face and her lips parted beneath him in an eager offering.

She loved the way he tasted.

Loved the texture of his lips.

The sweet mystery of his mouth.

Shyly, she ran her hands over his shoulders, gliding them over his shirt and sensing the hard bands of muscle beneath the cotton fabric. With trembling fingertips she stroked the back of his neck, thrilling to the heat of his burning skin.

'Mattie,' he whispered hoarsely into her mouth and she thought she might die of happiness.

Winding her arms around his neck, she felt every part of her begin to dissolve as she sank into a slow, dark meltdown.

'What's your problem, Jake? You look like you lost a dollar and found five cents.'

Jake flashed a smile at Roy. He'd been caught out, thinking about his parents, about how angry he was because, once again, they were too busy to come to Sydney to visit the man who'd been their head stockman for thirty years. Not that he'd share that news with Roy.

He shook his head. 'Don't start worrying about me, old-timer. I just want you to concentrate on getting well.'

Roy dismissed this with a wave of his hand. 'That's the doctors' job. Anyway, I'd recover a darn sight faster if I knew you'd stopped making such a dog's breakfast of your love life.'

Jake's jaw dropped so hard he was in danger of dislocation. 'Where did that come from?'

Roy gave a defensive shrug. 'I've been meaning to speak to you about it for a long time.'

'And since when have you been an expert on other people's love lives?'

'That's not the point. I'm an expert on *you*, Jake, and I know what makes you tick. I know what scares you about women.'

Something inside Jake cracked, but he did his resolute best to ignore it. 'Scared of women?' he said shakily. 'Have you any idea how many women I've dated?'

'Too many.' Roy's bottom lip protruded stubbornly.

'It's not possible to have too many women.' Jake's response was automatic, a reflex conditioned by years of carelessness, but now he could hear the hollow ring of dishonesty.

Since he'd met Mattie, he hadn't dated anyone else, hadn't even thought about other women, and that was a mighty scary state of affairs for a perennial bachelor.

Roy was watching him through narrowed eyes.

Jake scowled back at him. 'What does that look mean?'

'I'm thinking about that time after your brother was stillborn.'

The air around Jake solidified. He struggled to breathe.

Roy's hand patted Jake's forearm. 'After that baby died, your mother retreated from you, Jake. She pulled back from the world and spent six months lost under a black cloud. I don't know what they call it these days—depression, maybe—but, living in isolation in the Outback, she probably didn't get the help she needed. Your dad was worried sick about her. Neither of them could see what it was doing to you.'

'You're talking too much,' Jake said quietly. 'You're supposed to save your breath.'

'I feel I've got to say this,' Roy insisted. 'You see, I knew how it was before that baby died. You adored your mother. You had a wonderful relationship with her.'

Jake swallowed to ease the ache in his throat. 'After-wards, she couldn't look at me without crying.'

'Yeah, I know,' Roy said. 'And I watched you pull on your armour, like a brave little soldier. Shielding yourself from the pain.'

Jake's throat was so tight and sore he couldn't speak. For so many years, he'd blocked out these memories, but now Roy had stripped off their protective coverings. It was as if they were there sitting in front of him. Unavoidable.

'Then, just as your mother was recovering, they shunted you off to that boys' boarding school.' Roy sighed heavily. 'Since you were ten years old, you've lived in a world filled with males and you're still doing it, hiding away in Mongolia. Oh, yes, you date plenty of women, but you've never allowed yourself to get close. You don't want to get hurt.'

'Right now, I'm spending half my life in a maternity ward,' Jake said tersely.

'And it's scaring the life out of you.'

The pressure in Jake's lungs grew. His eyes stung. His throat burned. He gritted his teeth and clenched his hands as he fought for control.

'I'm not right for her,' he said stiffly.

There was no need to explain. Roy understood.

'You're perfect for Mattie.'

'Do you believe that? Honestly?' It was pathetic how badly he needed to hear this from the old man.

'I know it, Jake. And I know she's perfect for you. That's why you're so frightened.'

Jake sat very still beside the bed, staring at the veins on the backs of his hands, scarcely daring to breathe.

'You don't want to end up a lonely old codger like me, Jake.'

'But you chose to be a bachelor.'

This was greeted by a groaning chuckle.

'You never wanted to marry, did you?'

'It wasn't for lack of wanting.'

'What stopped you, then?'

'Couldn't work up the courage.'

'No.' The word came on a whispered breath. Jake couldn't believe his old hero had backed away from anything.

'Bravery's a funny thing,' Roy said softly. 'I could face a wild bull without a tremor, but I couldn't give my heart into a woman's keeping.'

His pale blue eyes regarded Jake gently. 'It's a danger, Jake. If you keep your heart under lock and key for too long, you end up terrified to let it see the light of day.'

Jake sat very still, his pulse slamming in his ears, his mind fixed on Mattie.

'She's such a good person.' It was little more than a whisper.

'And you're not a good person?' Roy croaked a disbelieving laugh. 'Come on, mate. Look at how well you've cared for me.'

'But that's because…' Jake stopped, unable to complete the sentence. He tried again. 'You were always there for me.'

'And Mattie will always be there for you too.' Roy's eyes gleamed softly. 'Give that girl half a chance and she'll let you keep her happy for the rest of her life.'

CHAPTER TEN

'BABY needs chocolate?' Mattie's eyes widened as she read the slogan stamped on the side of Jake's latest gift.

'These are special chocolate bars for pregnant mothers,' Jake told her proudly. 'The woman at Ready and Waiting assured me they're stacked with nourishment.'

Mattie laughed. 'The woman at Ready and Waiting must be your new best friend.'

'I'm certainly her new best customer.'

'And I'm one lucky pregnant woman.' Mattie lifted the lid. 'Ooh, the chocolate smells divine, Jake, thank you.'

She couldn't believe how fabulous this week had been.

Since their first in-house dinner together, Jake had visited her daily, sometimes twice daily, between his visits to Roy, and he'd brought all manner of lovely surprises from a special maternity store he'd unearthed in one of the bayside suburbs.

Such lovely gifts—expensive buttery creams for her skin, a silk-covered journal for her to record her memories.

'You're a writer and I thought you'd like to put the surrogacy experience into words,' he said.

A beautiful idea, she agreed. She'd write a journal for the babies to read in the future.

Jake had also brought all kinds of tempting, nourishing things to eat and sentimental movies Mattie could watch on her laptop.

'I know you prefer thrillers,' he said with a sweet, concerned expression that made her insides do cartwheels. 'But, considering your delicate condition, I thought you might prefer something less bloodthirsty.'

Of course, she hadn't admitted that she actually adored these gorgeous, soppy movies, but she wondered if Jake had guessed.

On several afternoons she'd completely lost herself in the lush romantic storylines of these films. Alone in this room, with the door closed, she'd wept and snuffled to her heart's content.

She'd never dreamed that Jake could be such an attentive and thoughtful hospital visitor. And she'd certainly never anticipated that such a gorgeous man could still make her feel attractive when her abdomen was the size of a harvest moon. Whenever Jake kissed her, he had to contend with a baby's knee or an elbow digging into him, but he didn't seem to mind.

If he was still upset about the surrogacy, he didn't show it.

Today, he was completely at ease. He quickly made himself at home, slumping into the chair beside her bed with his shoes off and his feet in socks, propped on the edge of her mattress. Mattie peeled away the paper wrapping on a maternity chocolate bar and took her first bite.

'Oh, yum.' She offered it to Jake. 'Try some.'

He took a bite from the place where her mouth had been. After he'd swallowed, he laughed. 'Thanks. I hope pregnancy isn't catching.'

They talked about Roy's impending operation and his

post-operative care. And Mattie told Jake that the latest scan showed that the babies had settled into an awkward position. The doctor was planning a Caesarean section for the week after next, or possibly sooner.

Jake quickly lost his casual pose. His face paled visibly. 'Do you mind having a Caesarean?'

'I can't wait.'

'Really?' His throat rippled as he swallowed and his face tightened into a worried smile. 'I suppose the bonus is that you won't have to go into labour.'

He seemed so nervous about the birth. Mattie supposed it was a guy thing. He'd mentioned that his mother had had pregnancy complications, so perhaps he had lingering fears.

To her surprise, she wasn't afraid at all. From the moment she'd started this project, she'd had really strong vibes that all would be well. 'I've been assured that Caesars leave very neat little scars,' she said, hoping to distract him.

He nodded, but he didn't look happy.

In the awkward silence she hunted for a safe subject, while Jake frowned and rolled a corner of her bed sheet between his fingers. She wondered if he was trying to find another topic too.

Without looking at her, he said, 'Have you given much thought to how you'll feel when this is finished? When you hand the babies over?'

Mattie swallowed a piece of chocolate too quickly. 'I've thought about little else,' she admitted. 'At times, the only thing that's kept me going is imagining the moment when Gina and Tom first hold their babies. I must have pictured their happy, goofy grins a thousand times.'

'But what about you, Mattie? Have you thought about how *you* will feel?'

'I'll be happy for Gina and Tom.'

With a heavy sigh, he let his head fall back and he stared at the ceiling. 'But how will you feel when Gina and Tom walk away with their babies?' He was still staring at the dull off-white paintwork. 'When they're off in a nursery somewhere, learning all about feeding regimes or whatever they have to learn, how will you feel when you're back in this room, all alone?'

With a flabby tummy and sore milky breasts?

Mattie felt as if the entire chocolate bar had lodged in her throat. She swallowed uncomfortably, but the sharp, tight ache remained. 'I haven't let myself worry about that. I've been concentrating on growing the babies and getting them safely delivered.'

His dark gaze skewered her. 'With no thought at all for yourself?'

'Not really.'

But, now that Jake had raised this question, Mattie found that she already knew the answer. She would feel abandoned, unnecessary, like an empty chrysalis after the butterfly had flown.

There was every chance she would need a shoulder to lean on, strong arms to hold her. But not just any shoulder, not just any arms.

Could she tell Jake that?

They'd made huge progress in a week. They'd talked about their families, their schooldays, their best friends, their pet hates, their favourite foods. They'd played Scrabble and backgammon and poker. They'd kissed and their kisses had been…unambiguous.

But they hadn't, until now, talked about the future, or where this newly hatched relationship was heading.

Now Jake's question had taken them into uncharted waters, but he'd relinquished the steering wheel. His eyes were shadowed and difficult to read as he waited for her answer.

Oh, heavens, if only she was braver. If only she couldn't remember so clearly how Pete had squirmed whenever she'd tried to talk about their future. In her most depressed moments, she'd wondered if Pete had only promised marriage to keep her quiet.

If she was too forward now, if she sounded the slightest bit pushy, she might send Jake running and she couldn't bear that.

She massaged an uncomfortable spot just below her breastbone where a little foot protruded. 'I guess I'll pick myself up and start all over again.' She forced brightness into her voice. 'Like the old song.'

'The way you did after your grandmother died?'

'Yes,' she said, pleased that he understood.

Jake, however, was watching her with a disconcerting frown. 'You've also had to get up again after being knocked down in a relationship, haven't you?'

Her jaw dropped in surprise. 'Does it show?'

He smiled sadly. 'There has to be a reason why a lovely, generous girl like you doesn't have half the men in Sydney knocking on her door.'

At first she could only stare at Jake while she savoured his compliment, but eventually she gathered her wits. 'Well, yes…I have wasted three years of my life over a boyfriend who said he wanted marriage and changed his mind at the last moment.'

Jake's frown deepened. 'Was it bad?'

'About as bad as it gets. It's pretty awful calling off a

wedding, selling a wedding gown you've never worn. Seeing all that pity in everyone's eyes.'

She held her breath as she waited for Jake's response. In the movies she'd been watching, at a precarious moment like this the hero drew the heroine into his arms and told her that he'd fallen madly in love with her, that he would never let her down.

At the very least, Jake could finally explain why he'd given up so much time and effort to entertain her.

But Jake didn't speak. He simply looked worried and strained, as if he was distinctly uncomfortable with such private revelations.

Mattie was awash with disappointment. This was his chance to explain why an unquestionably hunky bachelor, with his choice of thousands of available women, chose to spend hours and hours in a maternity ward with a woman who was not carrying his child.

But, although she waited, Jake didn't continue. In fact he avoided making eye contact and she could feel her heart sinking through the mattress.

'What about you, Jake?' She had to try again. 'How will you feel once the babies are handed over to Gina and Tom?'

'Relieved.'

Sadness lingered in his smile as he stood slowly and bent to kiss her cheek. His breath was warm against her ear.

'I suppose you'll be pleased when I'm no longer pregnant?' she asked hopefully.

With another sad smile, he tucked her hair behind her ear. 'I'll be very pleased and very relieved.' He pressed a kiss onto her lips and then he left to visit Roy.

He couldn't wait to get away, Mattie thought as she watched him go, but then *she* remembered why romantic movies always made her feel miserable and inadequate. In her world, the *real* world, divinely gorgeous men didn't sweep her into a powerful embrace and swear to love her till she drew her last breath.

In her life, the men made every show of loving her and then they moved on. To other women.

The hospital was dark when Mattie clambered out of bed, needing to go to the bathroom, as she did several times every night.

Fuzzy with sleep, she glanced at the bedside clock and saw the glowing green digits announcing that it was four forty-five. She fumbled in the dark for the bathroom door and one of the babies kicked a mean jab, low into her bladder.

Wincing, she pushed the door open, took a sleepy step forward onto the cool tiles.

Without warning, warm water gushed between her legs, splashing her nightgown and soaking her bare feet.

Her heart pounded as she stared at the puddle on the floor. She felt a leap of fear. Had she totally lost control of her bodily functions?

Then she realised what must have happened and her fear was overtaken by a hot flurry of excitement.

It was only just light. Jake was trying to stay in that happy limbo between sleeping and waking when his mobile phone let out a soft vibrating rumble.

Without raising his head, he felt around in the untidy heap of things beside the bed. 'Morning,' he mumbled into the phone.

'Jake?'

He sat bolt upright. 'Mattie, is that you?'

'I hope I haven't rung too early.' Her voice sounded different, as if she was scared or excited or maybe both.

'What is it? What's happened?'

'I'm going to have the babies this morning.'

The words hit him like a grenade exploding at close range. In that instant, he was wide-awake, facing every nightmare fear, every dark memory.

'Isn't this too soon?' he cried, fighting off waves of panic.

'It's a bit early, but my waters have broken so we don't really have much choice. But it's OK, Jake. Most twins come early.'

He was amazed that she could sound so calm. There was even a smile in her voice, an edge of exhilaration, like a climber who'd almost reached Everest's peak.

Jake's stomach twisted with fear.

'So where are you now?' he asked. *Stick to practical details. Keep those other thoughts at bay.*

'I'm still in my room.'

'I'll come and see you.' Already he was heading for the pile of clothes he'd dumped on a chair. 'I'm on my way.'

'But I'm not sure how much longer I'll be here.'

'Doesn't matter. I'll find you.'

He had to be there, had to see her. Maybe if he was there, if he stayed with Mattie, everything would be all right.

'Jake?' Her voice was tiny suddenly, but it shot like a dart straight into his heart.

'Yes?'

'I…' She hesitated and seemed to change her mind. 'Thanks for coming.'

'No worries, sweetheart. See you soon.' He disconnected and his heart pounded as he hunted for clothes.

The drive to the hospital was torture. The early morning

traffic was slow and every junction threw up a red light. Pedestrians crossed roads at a snail's pace. Throughout it all, Jake's stomach churned and his skin was clammy with fear. How would he cope if something happened to Mattie?

How could he help her if tragedy struck today? He owed her so much. She'd changed him. Until he'd met her, his life had been one-dimensional—focused on chasing money and good times. The main attraction of his work in Mongolia had been the automatic transfer of large chunks of money into his bank account.

Hell, he hadn't even been a proper environmentalist. He'd had a keen interest in the natural world, but he'd never become impassioned about any particular environmental issue. He'd been as shallow as a kids' wading pool.

No one was more surprised than he was by his behaviour in the past few weeks.

That was Mattie's doing. She brought out the best in him.

But, even with Roy's prompting, he'd still held back from telling her this. He still wasn't sure he could offer any promises. Had he left it too late to tell her how he felt?

Mattie heard the rumble of the trolley that would take her to Theatre and she took a deep breath. This was it.

Very soon she would no longer be pregnant, and Gina and Tom would be parents.

Her task was almost over.

And, somewhere out there in the busy Sydney streets, Jake was on his way.

She thought of the morning she'd driven him to the airport and the tearful farewell, when he'd told her he couldn't promise her a future with him.

How could she ever have guessed he'd be back in

Sydney again, visiting her daily, trying to be with her now as she faced this delivery?

Surely that meant he loved her?

How silly she'd been to doubt him. She'd been waiting for him to say the words, but she, Mattie Carey, knew better than most that actions spoke louder than words. Always.

Thank heavens she'd remembered this just in time.

She was smiling as the two orderlies came through her doorway, pushing the trolley between them.

At last Jake reached the hospital car park and, as he rushed along the walkway to the maternity ward, he tried to call Mattie again. His hands were shaking as he pressed her number. The phone rang and rang until her calm voice told him to leave a message after the beep.

It took forever for the lift to climb to her floor. Jake charged up the hall to her room.

It was empty.

He sagged against the door, expelling his breath in a huff of despair.

Where was she now?

A split-second later, he was rushing to the nurses' station.

The nurses on the maternity ward knew him by now and this morning the friendliest one, Beth, beamed at him.

'Where's Mattie?' he demanded.

'They've already taken her to Theatre.'

'Which way?' he cried. 'I've got to see her.'

Beth shook her head. 'I'm sorry, Jake. I don't think—'

'Don't try to stop me. I'm going to her! Please, just tell me the quickest way to find her.'

Beth's blue eyes widened and for several seconds she

stared at him, as if she was weighing his demands against hospital protocol.

'I've got to be there,' Jake urged through clenched teeth.

Beth swallowed.

'I love Mattie,' he said in a lowered, desperate whisper. 'But I haven't told her. You've got to help me.'

Her eyes were suddenly shiny. 'Right!' As if her doubts had vanished, she grabbed Jake roughly by the elbow. 'We've got to hurry. Come on, it's this way!'

To Jake's surprise, Beth ran with him all the way.

'You'll have to change into theatre clothes,' she ordered, shoving him through a doorway.

'I have to what?'

Her eyes were huge, her expression significant as she rounded on him. 'You want to be there with Mattie, don't you?'

'Inside? In the theatre?' He flinched from the thought. He'd been hoping to find Mattie in some kind of waiting area. 'I…I…'

For one treacherous moment he almost caved in. If he went inside, he would see the whole procedure—knives cutting into Mattie. Newborn babies.

Fear became a taste in the back of Jake's throat. A picture of his baby brother flashed before him, forcing him to see again that cold, tiny, lifeless face.

A wave of dizziness swept over him, but he knew he couldn't pull out of this now. He couldn't wait through another lonely vigil like the one that still haunted him. He couldn't leave Mattie alone.

Heaven alone knew what ordeal she faced but, whatever happened now, he had to be with her all the way.

Swallowing a glut of fear, he nodded to Beth. 'I want

to be with her.' He felt a small explosion in the middle of his chest. 'What do I have to do?'

'Hurry!' Beth shouted as she thrust a green theatre gown into his arms.

Beneath the bright theatre lights, Mattie felt alone and terrified. She hadn't expected to see so many gowned people in here—obstetricians, paediatricians, midwives, an anaesthetist. Not one friendly face, and not one of the people she needed most.

Jake had probably been held up in traffic. Gina and Tom were on their way from Willowbank, but they couldn't possibly make it in time, and not one of the friendly nurses from the maternity ward was here.

It might have helped if she'd been dosed with relaxing drugs, but nothing like that had been offered. Now, everything was happening too fast.

Already, the anaesthetist was asking her to roll over. He wanted to stick a needle into her spine. But it was too soon.

'Could you wait just a minute?' she muttered, but the anaesthetist took no notice. He rubbed her back with something cold and she felt the prick and sting of a needle. She pictured the anaesthetic sinking into her, spreading to her heart, her arteries, her veins. Soon the entire bottom half of her body would be numb.

'What happens now?' she asked, but everyone seemed too busy to answer her. Had they forgotten she was here?

Could someone smile? Please, don't ignore me.

The medical team began to erect a green cloth as a screen around her stomach. Mattie's heart raced. Any minute now the doctor would make his incision. This felt all wrong. It was too clinical. Like an operation. Not a birth.

Behind her a door crashed open.

'Oh, thank God,' cried a voice. 'We're not too late.'

Mattie turned her head and saw Beth's friendly face. And there was Jake!

Oh, gosh. Oh, wow! He looked wonderful. Familiar and yet strangely alien in a hospital cap and gown.

'Who's this?' Dr Smith, the obstetrician, looked up from whatever he was doing and fixed Jake with a steely stare.

Jake's face was unusually pale as he snapped to attention and took a step forward. 'I have to be with Mattie.'

'He's her boyfriend,' Beth announced and then she made a hasty amendment. 'Her partner.'

Dr Smith's grey eyes looked surprised but Jake was already standing at Mattie's right shoulder and he reached down and clasped her hand. 'I'm...I'm the surrogate father,' he said.

Several masked faces turned to look at Jake, amusement dancing in their eyes, but the doctor simply nodded, businesslike once more, as he turned his attention to Mattie's abdomen.

Mattie looked up into Jake's face and saw his heart shining in his eyes. She tried to speak, but a thousand emotions rose to fill her throat and she could only manage a strangled sob.

He smiled with aching tenderness as he bent down to her. 'Hi there.'

'Hey.'

He squeezed her hand. 'Just keep smiling, sweetheart.'

She was smiling straight into his eyes when she felt the cutting sensation on the other side of the screen. A flash of fear sliced through her, but Jake dipped his head and she felt the reassuring warmth of his lips on her brow.

There was a pulling sensation somewhere in her middle and suddenly a voice cried in triumph, 'It's a boy.'

Gloved hands held a baby high and Mattie saw his gleaming creamy skin, his perfect limbs and his little scrunched face, capped by dark, unmistakably red hair.

Her face broke into a broad grin. 'Oh, the little darling. He looks exactly like Tom.'

She heard Jake's abrupt laugh—half excited, half scared—and felt his hand gripping hers more tightly.

Already, another doctor was pulling out the little girl but, before Mattie could see her properly, she was whisked away.

'What's the matter?' Mattie called after them fearfully.

'Don't worry. She'll be all right,' Beth hastened to reassure them. 'She just needs resuscitation.'

'Can't she breathe?' Jake's voice was raspy and rough, as if he was scared too.

'She'll breathe. But there was always a chance the smaller baby would need help. It's why Dr Smith insisted on a Caesarean.'

'Are you sure she's OK?'

Beth patted Mattie's shoulder. 'I'm sure, honey, but I'll go and check for you. Be right back.'

It was all over.

Mattie's incision had been repaired. She'd been reassured that the baby girl was fine, although she needed careful monitoring and would stay in an incubator for the next twenty-four hours.

Jake had been outside, making the necessary phone calls, and now there wasn't a lot for him to do as he followed Mattie out of Theatre and into Recovery, where a male nurse hovered over her, watching her intently and taking her blood pressure every few seconds.

Or so it seemed.

Mattie looked bright and happy as she held up her end of the conversation with the nurse. It was Jake who was completely lost.

He felt dazed, like the time he'd been thrown from a horse and found himself on the hard ground, totally winded and looking at the world upside down.

It was so hard to believe he'd actually witnessed the successful birth of two brand-new tiny human beings.

They'd survived. Mattie had survived. None of his fears had been realised. He should be feeling euphoric.

Instead, he still felt tense. The excitement was over and the babies had vanished into some distant nursery where perhaps, even now, they were being met by their parents. This was it—the moment when Mattie had to face the fact that she was alone.

Lost? Needing him?

Yeah, sure. Right now she was chatting happily to the male nurse who apparently needed to know every last medical detail of her surrogacy. Jake watched her cheerful smile and the way she waved her expressive hands as she talked animatedly to this other guy and his tension grew claws, took a stranglehold.

He needed to be alone with her. There was so much he wanted to tell her, but he might as well grab a coffee, visit Roy, do anything rather than hang around here like a fifth wheel.

He took a step towards the trolley. 'Mattie?'

She stopped in mid-sentence and turned. Her eyes were shining. 'Hi, Jake,' she said as if she'd just remembered his presence.

'I thought I might push off now.'

'Oh.' The word fell from her lips softly and a flood of pink rushed into her cheeks. She looked worried, held out her hand to him. 'But I haven't thanked you.'

'I haven't done anything.'

'You have. You came. You were here.' The glow in her eyes took on a damp sheen. Her lower lip trembled. 'You were perfect. All along you've been perfect.' She spoke as if the nurse wasn't there listening to every word. 'And I've made so many terrible mistakes.'

Jake was sure he'd swallowed a golf ball. *Mistakes? What was she talking about?*

Beside them, the nurse cleared his throat and Mattie shot him a cool glance. 'Could you give us a moment, please, Ben?'

'I'm supposed to observe you.'

'I know, but this is important. Just for a moment.'

Ben gave a doubtful shrug. 'I'll just be outside, then.'

'Thanks.'

As soon as he'd gone Mattie took both of Jake's hands in hers. Her cheeks were flushed, her eyes too shiny and she was trembling.

'What's the matter?' Jake whispered. 'Should I call the nurse back?'

'No. I'm all right. It's just…I'm scared.'

'About the babies? They said the little girl's fine.'

She shook her head. 'Not that.' She spoke softly and he could barely make out the words. 'I want to apologise.'

This didn't make sense. 'Mattie, what are you talking about?'

She closed her eyes and took a deep shuddering breath. 'I didn't want to get too close to another man.'

'I understand, Mattie. It's OK.'

'But I need to explain why I stopped answering your e-mails. I was afraid of getting involved, then getting hurt again, and then I didn't tell you about the babies and of course you got a shock—and I turned you away. But, in spite of everything, you've been so good to me and—'

Tears trembled on her lashes. 'I'm sorry.'

'Sorry?' He was at once panicky and wanting to dance on air. 'I should be the one to apologise. I'm ashamed of the way I carried on about the surrogacy, but I was dealing with a terrible fear about what might happen.'

'Because of your mother's complications?'

He realised then that the ghost had been laid to rest and he could actually talk about it. 'My baby brother was still-born, you see. I was only nine years old and my mother was ill and I…I saw him. I held him.'

'Oh, Jake, you poor darling.' Mattie touched his cheek in the gentlest of caresses. 'It must have been incredibly hard for you to come here today.'

'I'm on top of the world now.' He smiled shakily. 'You've given your friends the most amazing gift. You're the most wonderful girl.'

She raised her face and looked gravely into his eyes. 'But I'm not the girl you met.'

A bubble of laughter burst in Jake's throat. 'I'm not the man you met.' He lifted her hand and pressed his lips to her fingers. 'The babies aren't the only ones who've grown over the past eight months. I feel like I'm twice the man I was. I've learned so much from you.'

At first she didn't respond, but then a small smile played at the corners of her mouth.

'I love you, Mattie.'

How good it felt to say those words out loud. Finally they sounded real. They *were* real.

They made her smile.

Such a beautiful, shining, radiant smile.

He covered her hands with his and felt his confidence grow. 'I've...er...heard you're on the lookout for a new mission now.'

'Oh, yes. I did say that.'

'I was wondering if you might take me on.'

Her eyes widened.

'As an ongoing project,' he clarified.

'As a boyfriend?'

Jake nodded.

'Are you talking long term?'

He didn't miss a beat. 'Very long term.'

'Not forever, Jake?'

He smiled. 'Why not?'

A cough sounded behind them. 'OK,' Ben said. 'I hate to break up the party, but—'

Jake held up his hand. 'Please, mate, give us one more minute.'

'I really need to take Mattie's blood pressure now. And then she's all yours.'

'Can't you take her blood pressure after I ask her to marry me?'

To Jake's relief, the other guy's face broke into a grin.

'Make it quick,' Ben said, still grinning as he backed out of the room.

Jake turned to Mattie. Her eyes were shining. She was so beautiful.

'I love you, Mattie,' he said again, leaning close so only she could hear. 'I need you in my life.'

She smiled.

'I need you as my wife. I promise I won't let you down. I want to keep you close for ever.'

Her smile broadened to a grin. 'That's exactly where I want to be.'

They were back in Mattie's room when Gina and Tom arrived, their arms filled with flowers and their faces split by enormous grins.

'Mattie,' Gina cried, rushing to hug her. 'The babies are so, so gorgeous. Thank you, darling. Thank you. Thank you. I'm afraid I can never really thank you enough.'

The next few minutes were very noisy and busy as everyone spoke at once about the birth and the babies.

'We're really excited about you two,' said Tom and he pumped Jake's hand and slapped him on the back. Then, before Mattie could question Tom, the ecstatic new parents left, hurrying back to the nursery.

Mattie looked at Jake. His hair was untidy, he hadn't shaved and his shirt was in need of an iron. He looked a little scruffy, just as he had on the day she'd first seen him, and she felt a delicious pang of longing.

Suddenly Gina was back. 'I almost forgot. This is for you.' She pressed a white envelope into Mattie's hand. 'As an extra thank you.' She winked and was gone.

Mattie looked at Jake. 'I hope they haven't been terribly extravagant. They've already given me so much.'

'Not half as much as you've given them,' he said with a quiet smile.

She opened the envelope and found a lovely thank-you card and a slip of paper. 'Oh, my goodness.' She gave a shocked little laugh. 'It's a voucher for a holiday.'

Jake grinned. 'Exactly what you need.'

'It's for two, Jake. A room and meals for two at a resort on Daydream Island.'

His grin deepened. 'Even better.'

'But how did Gina and Tom know?' Puzzlement vied with excitement at she pictured a holiday on a tropical island with her gorgeous pirate. 'How did they know about you? About us?'

'Will probably told them.'

'Will?' Mattie's jaw dropped. Now she was completely baffled. 'How does he fit into this?'

With a sheepish smile, Jake sat on the edge of her bed. 'While they were stitching you up, I ducked outside to make phone calls. I rang Roy. He sends his love, by the way. And I rang Will and told him about the babies.'

'But you didn't tell him about us, did you? You hadn't— we hadn't—'

A dark tide stained Jake's neck. 'And I asked Will if he'd—' He pressed his lips together and looked incredibly guilty. 'I told him that if all went well, I was going to need him some time in the next couple of months.'

'What for?'

'To be best man at our wedding.'

Mattie gasped.

'And then Will must have rung Gina and Tom,' Jake said. 'I'm sorry. Are you mad?'

She shook her head. How could she be mad? 'Will is the perfect choice,' she said. Everything in her life was perfect.

'You look tired,' Jake suggested, dropping a light kiss on her brow.

She *was* tired. Tired and a bit sore, now that the anaesthetic was wearing off, but so happy she didn't care about any of the discomfort.

'Stay with me?' She patted the bed beside her.

With a slow smile, Jake slipped off his shoes and stretched beside her. His arms encircled her and happiness flowed through her as he gently kissed the curve of her neck.

'Close your eyes,' he whispered.

She did as she was told and let the tiredness wash through her. 'I love you,' she told him.

'I love you too.' He nuzzled her ear. 'And I'm going to keep on loving you. For ever.'

Mattie sighed happily and she felt Jake's warmth surround her, felt his heartbeat strong and steady against her, and she fell asleep with a smile on her face.

EPILOGUE

WELCOME to Willowbank.

The white-painted sign stood proudly in a bed of blue and white agapanthus on the outskirts of town.

'*Ta-da!* This is my home town.' Mattie grinned at Jake. 'Not exactly a bustling metropolis.'

She drove on down the wide main street, divided in the middle by a strip of well-tended lawn with willow trees and brightly coloured garden beds. Either side of the street, rows of old-fashioned timber buildings housed a mix of traditional shops and trendy new fashion stores and cafés.

'I like it,' Jake said.

Mattie shot him a sideways glance. 'You don't have to be polite.'

'No, I mean it. There's something special about being in the bush. And this is the quintessential Australian country town.'

'Complete with the quintessential clock tower right in the middle.' Mattie laughed, pointing.

Jake grinned. 'And the quintessential old-timers, passing the time of day on a seat in the sun.'

'There's my old primary school,' she said as they passed a playground filled with yelling, laughing children.

'And the School of Arts where you stood on stage to recite *The Man from Snowy River.*'

'How did you know?'

'I went to a country primary school too, you know.'

'Of course you did.'

They shared a smile and Mattie felt the tummy-tumbling happiness that she always felt when Jake gave her a certain look.

They were on their way to Gina and Tom's for lunch. This evening they would stay with her parents and they would discuss wedding plans. It was all incredibly exciting.

'Slow down,' Jake said as they left the main part of town and drove past houses on acreage.

Mattie slowed and felt a catch in her throat when she saw the *For Sale* that had caught his attention.

'That's the McLaughlins' place,' she said, excited by the eager intensity in Jake's face. 'I heard they were retiring to the Gold Coast.'

'Do you know the house? Have you been inside?'

'Years ago. In primary school I was friends with their daughter, but I lost touch when she went away to boarding school. As I remember, it's a lovely old house.'

From the street, they could see a graceful federation-style home, set well back from the road and fronted by attractive gardens. Stately old gum trees shaded the lawn and a row of liquid ambers provided a screen from the neighbours.

'The land runs down to the river,' Mattie said. 'And there's a little jetty.'

'It's perfect,' Jake announced as if he'd already made a decision.

'Do you mean you'd like to live here?'

He smiled. 'Possibly.' Reaching out, he traced the outline of her ear with a fingertip. 'What do you think? Should we come back tomorrow and check it out?'

Mattie gulped. 'Are you serious? Do you really think we could live here in Willowbank?'

'Why not?'

'Would you be able to find work here?'

He grinned. 'Couldn't we live off the royalties from your books?'

'If you don't mind starving in a garret.'

He chuckled. 'Never mind. Every district has environmental issues. If all else fails, I'll set up my own business.'

Mattie rewarded him with a kiss. It seemed too good to be true that she and Jake might settle here, close to her friends and family, in this house that she'd always admired.

A new thought struck, making her gasp. 'I've just remembered.'

'What?'

'Oh, gosh. Oh, wow!'

'Mattie, for heaven's sake, what is it? Tell me.'

'There's a little cottage on the property, down near the creek. Old Mr McLaughlin, the grandfather, used to live there. I remember how he used to sit on the porch, looking out over the water.'

They stared at each other, eyes wide, and then they spoke in unison. 'Roy.'

Next instant they were smiling, laughing, hugging each other with excitement.

'Would you really want Roy to live with us?' Jake asked as she nestled her head on his shoulder.

'It would be perfect. I'd love it.'

'God, I love you.' He nuzzled her cheek. 'How did I ever get this lucky?'

Jake kissed her and the kiss was scrumptious and lasted for ages, but eventually Mattie pulled away. 'I'm afraid we'd better get going. We don't want to be late for lunch.'

She turned off the main road and headed down the winding road that led through a grove of pines to Gina and Tom's farmhouse.

As they emerged onto the sun-dappled drive in front of the house, Tom was already coming down the steps with a grin as wide as a watermelon slice and little red-headed Jasper curled in his arms like a sleepy ginger-topped possum.

'So good to see you,' he said enthusiastically, kissing Mattie's cheek and shaking Jake's hand and congratulating them both, yet again, on their engagement.

Mattie gazed fondly at Jasper and found it hard to believe that he'd been inside her for all those months. 'How is he, Tom?'

'Settled at last, thank heavens, but he kicked up quite a stink this morning.' Tom grinned and his eyes glowed with unmistakable pride. 'He didn't want to miss the party.'

'And Mia?'

'Sound asleep. She's the model child.'

'The darling.'

Jake retrieved the hamper of gourmet delicacies that he and Mattie had scoured Sydney's delis to find and they went inside the big farmhouse kitchen, which was fragrant as ever with wonderful baking smells.

More laughter and congratulations followed as they greeted Gina.

'And Jake must meet Lucy,' Mattie said, beckoning her petite blonde friend closer. 'Jake, Lucy is Willowbank's favourite vet but, more importantly, she's going to be one of my bridesmaids.'

Lucy was smiling as she shook Jake's hand. 'Pleased to meet you,' she said demurely, but her eyes were sparkling as she turned to Mattie. 'Very impressive,' she whispered out of the corner of her mouth.

Gina beamed at everyone. 'We only need Will here now and we'd have everybody together.'

'He'll be back from Mongolia in time for the wedding,' Mattie told her. 'He's going to be Jake's best man.'

Lucy's sudden shocked gasp cut through the group's excitement. Everyone turned to stare at her and bright colour flooded her face.

She gave a self-conscious shrug and an awkward smile. 'Sorry. I…I hadn't heard that Will would be in the wedding party.'

'Is that a problem?' asked Jake, looking puzzled.

'No.' Lucy was recovering quickly, but her cheeks were still bright pink. 'No, of course not. It's no problem at all.'

Mattie wished she'd explained to Jake that Lucy and Will had a history. They'd been best friends at high school and they'd gone away to university together. Mattie had wondered if their friendship might grow into something deeper, but it never had.

She had never suspected any unfinished business between them. Now, she wasn't so sure.

Lucy, however, was clearly determined to make everyone forget her slip. 'It's so exciting that the wedding is only three months away, Mattie. I can't wait to help you with the planning.'

'It's going to be fun, isn't it?' Gina agreed. 'I do love weddings.'

'I can just see it now.' Lucy smiled dreamily. 'Mattie will look so beautiful.'

'Jake will look beautiful too,' Gina added with a cheeky wink.

'I say this calls for a drink,' Tom announced before the girls could get too carried away.

'Great idea.' Lucy was back to her usual bouncy self. 'I've brought a bottle of bubbly. Let's crack it open.'

The cork popped loudly, icy wine flowed and glasses clinked.

Happy voices cried, 'Here's to Mattie and Jake!'

Mattie caught Jake's eye. Months ago, she'd dreamed of a lovely gathering like this, where she and her best friends and Jake were together. She'd thought it was impossible.

Now, Jake sent her a smile and she read the clear message in his flashing dark eyes. They were a team and, together, everything was possible.

0609 Gen Std HB

MILLS & BOON®
Pure reading pleasure™

JULY 2009 HARDBACK TITLES

ROMANCE

Marchese's Forgotten Bride	Michelle Rei
The Brazilian Millionaire's Love-Child	Anne Mathe
Powerful Greek, Unworldly Wife	Sarah Morga
The Virgin Secretary's Impossible Boss	Carole Mortime
Kyriakis's Innocent Mistress	Diana Hamilto
Rich, Ruthless and Secretly Royal	Robyn Donal
Spanish Aristocrat, Forced Bride	India Gre
Kept for Her Baby	Kate Walke
The Costanzo Baby Secret	Catherine Spence
The Mediterranean's Wife by Contract	Kathryn Ros
Claimed: Secret Royal Son	Marion Lenno
Expecting Miracle Twins	Barbara Hanna
A Trip with the Tycoon	Nicola Mars
Invitation to the Boss's Ball	Fiona Harpe
Keeping Her Baby's Secret	Raye Morga
Memo: The Billionaire's Proposal	Melissa McClon
Secret Sheikh, Secret Baby	Carol Marinel
The Playboy Doctor's Surprise Proposal	Anne Frase

HISTORICAL

The Piratical Miss Ravenhurst	Louise Alle
His Forbidden Liaison	Joanna Maitlan
An Innocent Debutante in Hanover Square	Anne Herri

MEDICAL™

Pregnant Midwife: Father Needed	Fiona McArthu
His Baby Bombshell	Jessica Matthew
Found: A Mother for His Son	Dianne Drak
Hired: GP and Wife	Judy Campbe

0609 Gen Std LP

MILLS & BOON®
Pure reading pleasure™

JULY 2009 LARGE PRINT TITLES

ROMANCE

Captive At The Sicilian Billionaire's Command — Penny Jordan
The Greek's Million-Dollar Baby Bargain — Julia James
Wedded for the Spaniard's Pleasure — Carole Mortimer
At the Argentinean Billionaire's Bidding — India Grey
Italian Groom, Princess Bride — Rebecca Winters
Falling for her Convenient Husband — Jessica Steele
Cinderella's Wedding Wish — Jessica Hart
The Rebel Heir's Bride — Patricia Thayer

HISTORICAL

The Rake's Defiant Mistress — Mary Brendan
The Viscount Claims His Bride — Bronwyn Scott
The Major and the Country Miss — Dorothy Elbury

MEDICAL™

The Greek Doctor's New-Year Baby — Kate Hardy
The Heart Surgeon's Secret Child — Meredith Webber
The Midwife's Little Miracle — Fiona McArthur
The Single Dad's New-Year Bride — Amy Andrews
The Wife He's Been Waiting For — Dianne Drake
Posh Doc Claims His Bride — Anne Fraser

AUGUST 2009 HARDBACK TITLES

ROMANCE

Desert Prince, Bride of Innocence	Lynne Graham
Raffaele: Taming His Tempestuous Virgin	Sandra Marton
The Italian Billionaire's Secretary Mistress	Sharon Kendrick
Bride, Bought and Paid For	Helen Bianchin
Hired for the Boss's Bedroom	Cathy Williams
The Christmas Love-Child	Jennie Lucas
Mistress to the Merciless Millionaire	Abby Green
Italian Boss, Proud Miss Prim	Susan Stephens
Proud Revenge, Passionate Wedlock	Janette Kenny
The Buenos Aires Marriage Deal	Maggie Cox
Betrothed: To the People's Prince	Marion Lennox
The Bridesmaid's Baby	Barbara Hannay
The Greek's Long-Lost Son	Rebecca Winters
His Housekeeper Bride	Melissa James
A Princess for Christmas	Shirley Jump
The Frenchman's Plain-Jane Project	Myrna Mackenzie
Italian Doctor, Dream Proposal	Margaret McDonagh
Marriage Reunited: Baby on the Way	Sharon Archer

HISTORICAL

The Brigadier's Daughter	Catherine March
The Wicked Baron	Sarah Mallory
His Runaway Maiden	June Francis

MEDICAL™

Wanted: A Father for her Twins	Emily Forbes
Bride on the Children's Ward	Lucy Clark
The Rebel of Penhally Bay	Caroline Anderson
Marrying the Playboy Doctor	Laura Iding

0709 Gen Std LP

MILLS & BOON

AUGUST 2009 LARGE PRINT TITLES

ROMANCE

he Spanish Billionaire's Pregnant Wife	Lynne Graham
he Italian's Ruthless Marriage Command	Helen Bianchin
he Brunelli Baby Bargain	Kim Lawrence
he French Tycoon's Pregnant Mistress	Abby Green
iamond in the Rough	Diana Palmer
ecret Baby, Surprise Parents	Liz Fielding
he Rebel King	Melissa James
ine-to-Five Bride	Jennie Adams

HISTORICAL

he Disgraceful Mr Ravenhurst	Louise Allen
he Duke's Cinderella Bride	Carole Mortimer
mpoverished Miss, Convenient Wife	Michelle Styles

MEDICAL™

hildren's Doctor, Society Bride	Joanna Neil
he Heart Surgeon's Baby Surprise	Meredith Webber
Wife for the Baby Doctor	Josie Metcalfe
he Royal Doctor's Bride	Jessica Matthews
utback Doctor, English Bride	Leah Martyn
urgeon Boss, Surprise Dad	Janice Lynn